Alaskan Alliance

by

Kathi Daley

This book is dedicated to Bruce Curran, who exorcised the demons from my computer so that I didn't have to miss a single day of writing. Thank you, Bruce.

I also want to thank the very talented Jessica Fischer for the cover art.

And special thanks to Jade Knueppel, Joanne Kocourek, Michele Gray, Janel Flynn, and Amy Brantley for submitting recipes.

I also want to offer my gratitude to all the readers who helped me figure out a name for Whiskey, the awesome cat who lives in the bar. I had a ton of wonderful suggestions but decided to narrow it down to names suggested by Charlene Soreff, Wanda Philmon Downs, Betsy Anderson McAvoy, Amy Wright Johnson, and Michelle Thomas.

And, of course, thanks to the readers and bloggers in my life who make doing what I do possible.

And, as always, love and thanks to my sister Christy for her time, encouragement, and unwavering support. I also want to thank Carrie, Cristin, Brennen, and Danny for the Facebook shares, Randy Ladenheim-Gil for the editing, and, last but not least, my super-husband Ken for allowing me time to write by taking care of everything else.

Books by Kathi Daley

Come for the murder, stay for the romance.

Buy them on Amazon today.

Zoe Donovan Cozy Mystery:

Halloween Hijinks
The Trouble With Turkeys
Christmas Crazy
Cupid's Curse
Big Bunny Bump-off
Beach Blanket Barbie
Maui Madness
Derby Divas
Haunted Hamlet
Turkeys, Tuxes, and Tabbies
Christmas Cozy
Alaskan Alliance
Shamrock Shenanigans – *March 2015*

Books by Kathi Daley

Come for the murder, stay for the romance.
Buy them on Amazon today.

Paradise Lake Cozy Mystery:
Pumpkins in Paradise
Snowmen in Paradise
Bikinis in Paradise
Christmas in Paradise
Puppies in Paradise – *February 2015*

Whales and Tails Cozy Mystery:
Romeow and Juliet – *January 2015*

Road to Christmas Romance:
Road to Christmas Past

Chapter 1

Friday, December 26

The last thing any of us wants is to get a call from the hospital letting us know that someone we love has been involved in an automobile accident. In fact, I'm going to go out on a limb and say that this particular call ranks among the top of all the phone calls I really hoped never to receive. The snow was heavy today, and I could see how this type of thing could happen. The roads that can be found in and around Ashton Falls, the small mountain hamlet I call home, are narrow and winding, and the town is filled to the brim with tourists who have driven up from the valley for the week to enjoy a magical white Christmas. Add the stormy weather to the fact that very few of the visitors who come to our area are really prepared for severe winter driving and you have a recipe for disaster.

The thing is, according to my good friend, Dr. Ryder Westlake, who called me with the bad news, the accident that had occurred during the early morning hours hadn't been an accident at all. As I carefully made my way through the tourist-filled town, I had to ask myself who would intentionally run innocent people off the road in the middle of what was quickly becoming a New Year's week blizzard.

"How are they?" I asked as I slid in through the door of the hospital after slipping on a sheet of ice.

"Whoa, careful." Dr. Westlake grabbed my arm and steadied me. "We don't need another friend with broken bones."

"Broken bones?" I felt my heart skip a beat. "How bad is it?"

"I'm afraid your friends are beat up a bit, but both will be fine. Where's Zak?" Dr. Westlake referred to my fiancé, Zak Zimmerman, who was out of town for the day. "I hoped he'd be with you."

"He had to go out of town, but he should be back this evening if the weather allows. Levi, Ellie, Zak, and I are all supposed to go to Alaska tomorrow."

"I'm afraid Levi and Ellie won't be going anywhere except home to rest. Assuming you're able to give them a ride. Neither can drive."

Uh-oh. That didn't sound good at all. Levi Denton and Ellie Davis have been my best friends since kindergarten. While the three of us have established a solid best friend triad, I'm pretty sure that has officially developed into a couple—Levi and Ellie— and their best friend (me, Zoe Donovan).

"I have my truck. And I can call my dad to bring his Expedition," I offered.

"That might be a good idea."

"Do you know what happened?"

"I don't have all the details. Levi is madder than a cat in hot mud, though. I overheard him telling Sheriff Salinger that he was taking Ellie to breakfast early this morning when a large black truck heading in the opposite direction swerved toward them, causing them to run off the road and into a tree. Ellie has a broken right leg as well as abrasions on her right arm. Levi must have reached his right arm out to brace her when he saw the impact was imminent because he ended up with a broken right arm. The breaks are clean and I anticipate quick recoveries, but they're going to need someone to keep an eye on them for the first twenty-four hours at least."

"I'll take them to Zak's house. I'll make sure they rest," I promised.

"That would be perfect. I have a feeling they'll both wake up in the morning feeling like they were run off the road by a large black pickup."

"Do we know who was driving the truck that ran them off the road?" I asked.

"No," Dr. Westlake answered, "but Sheriff Salinger thinks it might have been fleeing the scene of the fire."

"Fire? What fire?" I asked.

"I'm sorry; I thought you'd heard. Someone set Buck Stevenson's lumberyard on fire this morning. Most of the damage was to the office and warehouse, but if there hadn't been as much snow on the ground as there is, it could have been a real disaster."

I frowned. I hadn't heard anything about the fire, but I'd slept in that morning because the previous forty-eight hours had been a very long two days. I couldn't imagine who would set fire to the lumberyard, but I did know that I didn't like the sound of anything that had occurred. Buck Stevenson was new to Ashton Falls. He'd bought the lumberyard less than a year ago but had quickly become a respected member of the community in spite of the fact that he'd spent a good long time in prison for killing a man in a tavern fight before moving to the lake.

"Can I see them?" I asked.

"Yeah; they're ready to go whenever you can arrange for transportation. Ellie is in exam room three and Levi is in room five."

I called my dad and asked if he could come to the hospital and help transport my friends to Zak's house. He was, of course, happy to do so. I headed toward Ellie's room after making the arrangements. I wanted to be there for both of my friends, but I knew that of the two, Ellie would be in the greatest need of a best friend's shoulder to lean on.

Most would say I'm used to seeing people in various states of ill health. My dog Charlie volunteers at the hospital as a therapy dog, so I spend more time than most within the walls of the large log building. I knew that if Levi's car had been struck on the right and Ellie was the passenger she would have suffered the brunt of the impact. I took a deep breath before entering her room, preparing myself for whatever it was I might find.

"Oh, Ellie," I cried as I hurried to her side. Her right leg was in a cast and her right arm was bandaged from the elbow down. She had a cut over her right eye, and it looked like she was going to have one heck of a bruise on her swollen cheek.

"How's Levi?" she asked the minute I entered the room.

"I haven't seen him," I admitted. "I stopped by here first."

"The nurses keep telling me he's fine, but they won't let me see him."

"Dr. Westlake has cleared you both to come home with me. My dad is on his way with the Expedition. What happened?"

"I don't know; it all happened so fast. We were driving along the highway and this big black truck swerved right into us. Levi cranked the wheel to avoid a head-on and we ran into a tree. The stupid truck never even slowed down."

"Did you recognize the driver?" I wondered.

Ellie frowned. "I'm not sure. He wasn't someone I know well, but he did look familiar. I'm sure I've seen him somewhere before. I just can't quite place where."

"Do you know what kind of a truck it was?"

Ellie thought about it. "It happened really fast. I didn't even see it coming. It was a large truck. An extra cab, I think. I'm going to guess domestic, but I can't say if it was a Dodge, a Chevy, or a Ford. Levi was driving, so he was watching the road as well as oncoming traffic, whereas I wasn't really paying attention to the road. I'd be willing to bet he can tell you more about it."

"I'll go check on him and see the nurse about your paperwork. I'll be back with a wheelchair as soon as my dad gets here, which should be just a few minutes now."

"Tell him to hurry. I hate being in this place."

"I know. He will. I'll be right back. I promise."

It took a while for the hospital staff to get the release paperwork together, so by the time I got my friends back to Zak's lakefront home it was time to do something about lunch. Luckily, we had leftovers from the Christmas holiday. A lot of leftovers. Not only had Zak cooked up a storm on Christmas Eve but our guests had brought food to share, and my mom had sent leftovers home from our Christmas Day dinner. That meant that there were plenty of already prepared choices; all I needed to do was heat stuff up.

"I'm not sure I can eat," Ellie said. "My stomach is still a little oogy."

"Dr. Westlake said you needed to take your pills with food, so try to eat a little. I can make you something else if you want."

"The turkey sandwich is fine." Ellie took a small bite.

"It seems like such a waste of time to be sitting here when the guy who tried to kill us is still out there," Levi insisted. "We need to come up with a plan."

"You were just in a major accident. Your 4Runner was totaled. Dr. Westlake has prescribed rest. I'm afraid you really need to let Salinger handle this," I counseled.

"Would you?" Levi asked. "If it were you and Zak in the accident would you sit idly by and let Salinger handle things?"

I hesitated.

"Be honest," Levi challenged me.

"No," I admitted. "I wouldn't sit around and wait for Salinger, but Dr. Westlake prescribed rest. For both of you." I glanced at Ellie and willed Levi to get my point. I hoped if he wouldn't rest for himself, he'd rest for the woman he loved. We both knew if he set out sleuthing there was no way Ellie would want to stay behind.

"Yeah." Levi sighed. "Okay. We can give Salinger a day or two to see what he can come up with."

"We need to call Jake to let him know that there's been a change in plans," I addressed Ellie, who had eaten most of her sandwich.

Levi, Ellie, Zak, and I were all supposed to leave for Alaska the following day to deliver a Search and Rescue dog to a team in Moosehead, Alaska. The team had recently had to retire the dog they had been working with after he was injured in a rescue.

"Levi and I obviously can't go to Alaska, but you need to," Ellie insisted. "The S and R team is counting on you. Peter is counting on you."

Peter Darwin was a dog trainer who had spent the last six months training Sitka, the golden retriever who was sitting at my feet, looking at me as if he knew he was the subject of our conversation. Sitka had been trained to serve as a search and rescue dog with a specialty in locating avalanche victims. The dog was worth thousands of dollars, so when Peter had a family emergency and was unable to deliver him to his new team himself, he'd asked me to do it. We'd spent part of the day on Christmas Eve going over the specialty commands and responses.

"But I need to stay here to take care of the two of you," I argued.

"We'll be fine," Ellie insisted. She looked at Levi. "Won't we?"

"Uh, yeah. Sure. Although," he looked at Ellie, "it would be nice to have Zoe's help finding the guy who did this to us."

Ellie gave Levi a look he seemed to understand because the next thing out of his mouth was, "Of course, delivering Sitka is important as well. You should go. Zak too. Ellie and I will be fine."

I hesitated. The last thing I wanted to do was leave my best friends at a time like this, but I'd promised Peter I'd deliver the dog, and from what I'd heard, the team in Moosehead was desperate to get him.

"I've already asked Tiffany to stay at the house to watch the animals," I said. "I guess she wouldn't mind taking care of the two of you as well."

"That would be perfect," Ellie responded.

It appeared as if Levi wanted to argue, but he glanced at Ellie again and then seemed to reconcile himself to the fact that Zak and I were going to Alaska.

"I'll deliver Sitka and then come back to Ashton Falls as soon as I can," I promised. "In the meantime, why don't we see what we can figure out about the truck that hit you? The more facts Salinger has to work with, the better the likelihood that he'll find the guy."

"When is Zak supposed to be back from delivering the kids to Scooter's grandparents?" Levi asked.

"Not until this evening. I'm sure he wanted to visit with the grandparents for a while to make sure Scooter and Alex were all settled in before heading back," I answered.

Scooter was a nine-year-old boy and Alex a nine-year-old girl who had spent Christmas with Zak and me. They both attended boarding school on the East Coast, but Scooter's grandparents, who lived on a farm in Kansas, had decided they wanted a few days with their grandchild before he went back to school for the winter semester.

"It'd be nice to have his computer hacking skills, but I suppose we can start with what we have," Levi said.

"After you eat your lunch and take your pills," I instructed. Levi glared at me, but I sensed he was going to play along. I felt bad for him. There was nothing worse than being the patient and sitting idly by when you felt an uncontrollable urge to take charge of your own situation.

I decided to excuse myself while Levi and Ellie ate in order to go upstairs to call Sheriff Salinger. We seemed to be getting along pretty well lately and I wanted to see if he would share what he knew and stay in contact with me while I was gone in the hopes that things would move along quickly enough to pacify Levi. Dr. Westlake had ordered rest, so the last thing I needed was to have to tackle my best friend to keep him from charging back out to take down the man who'd caused the accident.

"I was wondering how long it would take you to get in touch," Salinger answered the phone before I could even greet the man. "I rather thought you'd stop by, though."

I explained that I was currently playing nurse for my two injured friends. "I did hope you could fill me in on what, if anything, you know."

"I don't know a lot at this point."

"I know, but whatever you do know would help."

I waited while Sheriff Salinger made up his mind whether to share or not. Our relationship had started off on a rocky note fourteen months ago, when he'd had me fired from my job for doing his job when he seemed to be unable to make any progress on the investigation into the murder of a rival team's football coach. Since then we'd worked on more murder investigations than I'd like to admit to, and we've developed something of a symbiotic relationship.

"Levi Denton and Ellie Davis were run off the road at approximately six forty a.m. by a black Ford F-250. I believe the driver was fleeing the scene of a fire he'd just set at the lumberyard," Salinger began. "I don't know for certain why the man set the fire, but it appears that Buck Stevenson's office was the primary target, so we're assuming the office contained some sort of information the arsonist wanted to destroy. Mr. Stevenson was out of town for the Christmas holiday but has been located and is expected back later this afternoon."

"And the damage to the yard?" I asked.

"Minor, considering the potential for a huge fire with all that wood. I'm certain we would have had a much larger problem if we hadn't gotten so much snow during the past month."

"Any suspects?" I asked.

"We have a list of black F-250 owners we're tracking down. We should be able to narrow things down a bit further once we interview Mr. Stevenson."

I took a few extra minutes to explain that I needed to go to Alaska for a few days and was worried that Levi would take matters into his own hands. Salinger assured me that he would keep an eye on Levi, which concerned me even more. Levi and Salinger don't have the best of relationships, due mostly to the fact that my friend has been the prime suspect in more than one of Ashton Falls' recent rash of murders.

After I got off the phone with Salinger I made sure Levi and Ellie took the pills Dr. Westlake had given me. Surprisingly, when I suggested they lay down for a bit they both agreed and quickly fell asleep on the big guest bed in one of the downstairs bedrooms. By the time they woke up it was already dark, and Zak was on his way up the mountain from the airport in the valley. I made us some dinner while the new couple helped each other change into the clean clothes I'd gathered for them while they slept.

"What smells so good?" Zak asked as he walked through the back door into the kitchen.

"I'm heating up the soup that was in the freezer," I answered before kissing him in greeting. "I'm going to make some garlic bread to go with it."

"Great. I'm starving and totally beat. All I want to do is eat something and then go to bed and sleep until it's time to leave for the airport tomorrow."

"Yeah, about that . . ." I explained about the accident and the fact that Levi and Ellie were staying at the house. "They slept most of the day and I'm afraid they're all geared up to do some investigation into the identity of the man in the black truck. They want you to look up some things on the Internet and have been anxiously awaiting your arrival."

Zak groaned and then smiled tiredly. "Of course I want to help in any way I can. I'm going to take the backstairs up and take a shower. You'd better put on some coffee. Strong coffee," he clarified.

Chapter 2

Saturday, December 27

I clung tightly to Charlie as the private jet that brought us to Alaska prepared for descent into the tiny airport in Moosehead. The dark sky took on an eerie glow from the airport lights, but the snow had become so heavy that I couldn't see anything outside the small window next to me. Zak must have noticed my trepidation and squeezed my shoulder in a show of support.

"It's going to get bumpy," the pilot, Coop, informed us through the intercom system that provided communication between the cockpit and the passenger lounge.

"Oh, great." I tried to smile. "Bumpy. How fun."

"You'd better secure Sitka and Charlie in their crates and fasten your seat belts," Coop added. "It looks like we have a major storm front working its way into the area."

I hated to let go of Charlie, preferring to find comfort in his warm and furry body, but Coop was right. He would be safer in the crate, which secured so that it couldn't roll around. Sitka went happily into his crate, having been trained to enjoy time in it, but Charlie was a lapdog and had spent very little time in his own dungeon of confinement. He was, however, well trained, so he went into the crate when instructed, though I had to look away as he glanced at me with a sad face that begged me to rescue him. As soon as the dogs were secure, Zak sat back down next to me. We both fastened our seat belts and then held on for the bumpy arrival on the small, single runway.

"It's going to be fine," Zak assured me.

"I know," I told him as I dug my nails into his leg.

"Coop is a pro. He's flown in much worse weather than this."

"I know."

Zak removed my hand from his leg and entwined his fingers with mine. I'm pretty sure his gesture was more about the craters I was digging in his leg than anything else, but it was nice to hold his hand. I'd flown in the small jet Zak chartered several times since he and I began dating, but I'd never experienced anything quite as terrifying as the landing that evening. I let out the breath I'd been holding since we began our descent when the wheels finally touched down on the snow-covered surface after the aircraft rocked back and forth multiple times as Coop struggled to land it in the high winds.

"I think I'm going to puke."

"Take a deep breath in through your nose and then out through your mouth," Zak encouraged.

I did as instructed.

"Again." Zak took several long, deep breaths along with me, in order, I imagine, to give me something to focus on other than the delayed shock caused by my certainty of imminent death.

"Better?" he asked.

"Yeah, thanks." I let the dogs out of the crates as the jet taxied to the small terminal. Sitka and Charlie both seemed relieved to be on the ground as well;

they paced around excitedly as Zak gathered our luggage.

The moment the exterior door opened the dogs ran toward the fresh air. Charlie waited for me to make my way over to him, but Sitka jumped out of the now parked aircraft and ran across the tarmac. Before I could call him back he jumped on a person dressed in a red parka and tackled her to the ground.

"Sitka," I screamed in horror. I ran down the stairs, which had been lowered, and across the pavement with Charlie barking at my heels. "Sitka, come," I called again.

By the time I reached the dog and the person who was still pinned to the ground I was totally out of breath. "Sitka, off," I commanded in my most commanding voice. Sitka looked at me and obeyed. I lent a hand to the woman on the ground. "I'm so sorry. I have no idea what came over him."

"It's okay." The girl laughed. "He was just happy to see me."

For the first time I realized that Sitka had been wagging his tail and licking the girl's face and not attacking her, as I had thought.

"You know Sitka?"

"I raised him for the first six months of his life. My name is Harmony." The girl stuck out her hand in a gesture of greeting.

"I'm glad to meet you too, and very glad Sitka wasn't eating you." There was something immediately likable about the girl. I'm not sure if it was the laughter in her dark eyes or the fact that she had dog kisses all over her face and wasn't even trying to wipe them off. "The silly dog gave me a heart attack. I thought for certain he'd attacked you."

The girl's hood fell off, revealing long dark hair as she bent over and hugged the dog. "I'm sure the big lug just missed me, which makes me happy because I was certain he would have forgotten me while he'd been away for training."

"Apparently he was looking for you. He must have realized where we were and expected to find you; he was out the door the minute it opened." I frowned. "I thought Peter said someone named Jake was Sitka's owner and handler."

"He is. I lived with Jake when Sitka was a puppy, so he and I became friends. I'll explain everything to you on the way to Neverland."

"Neverland?" I asked.

"Neverland is the name of the tavern Jake owns. Jake sent me with the van. He's out on a rescue or he would have come himself."

I looked back to where Coop was handing our luggage down to Zak.

"The weather is going to get bad in a very short amount of time, so your pilot should fuel up and be on his way if he cares about getting out of here anytime soon," Harmony continued. "They say the storm that's rolling in could last for several days at least."

I turned around and waved at Zak. "I'll let him know. By the way, this is Charlie," I introduced my dog.

"I'm happy to meet you, Charlie."

Based on the look of adoration on Charlie's face he'd found a new friend. I looked at my little buddy and smiled. It always made me happy to see Charlie happy.

"Charlie, stay with Harmony," I instructed. "I'll get Zak and be right back."

Charlie seemed to understand what I wanted him to do because he sat obediently at Harmony's feet. She didn't even seem to notice that her dark hair was covered with snow as she squatted down to chat with both dogs while I made my way back to the plane. There are times when you know right away that you've found a kindred spirit. I'd barely spoken two sentences to the girl, but I'd bet a month's wages that we were going to end up the best of friends.

Which reminded me of my best friends back in Ashton Falls. I'd need to be sure to call them once we got settled. I knew Tiffany would take good care of them, but in spite of the fact that they'd both encouraged me to make the trip as planned, I felt bad about leaving them in their time of need.

After loading the dogs and the luggage, Zak climbed into the backseat of the large yellow van while I got into the passenger seat in the front. Within minutes Zak was sound asleep. Poor guy really had been through a long couple of days. Christmas Day had begun when the kids got up before dawn after we'd had a late night putting together bikes. The early morning had been followed by a long day of sugared-up preteens running around having the time of their lives while they tried out each of their gifts. And finally, we'd enjoyed a late night visiting with my parents, talking about our plans for the future after enjoying the delicious meal they'd prepared.

And then Zak had gotten up before sunrise to take Scooter and Alex to Kansas to spend time with his grandparents before they returned to school for the winter semester. By the time he returned to Ashton

Falls that evening his eyes had been at half-mast, and I know he was looking forward to a good long sleep, but instead he'd spent hours discussing options when he'd found out what had happened to Levi and Ellie. After another very late night he'd had to get up early this morning to drive down the mountain to catch the plane that would take us to Alaska. No wonder he was so tired.

"You certainly have a brightly colored van," I commented.

"It's bright to provide visibility during a whiteout or on a dark winter night. Trust me, you haven't seen dark until you've seen Alaska dark."

"That makes sense, actually. So you live with Jake?" I asked as we drove away from the airport toward the tavern and grill where we were supposed to meet up with Jake and the rest of the Search and Rescue crew.

"My parents died when I was thirteen and my sister Valerie was eighteen," Harmony began.

"I'm so sorry."

"Thank you. It was a long time ago, but it still stings a bit, if you know what I mean."

I think I did; although both of my parents were alive and well, I had lost my grandmother, who'd help raise me when my mom left.

"Long story short, because Val was eighteen the courts allowed her to be my legal guardian," Harmony continued. "When she was twenty she married Jake, who she'd been dating since high school. We moved in with him and were all very happy. When Val was twenty-two she died during a rescue. I was seventeen at the time and had no other family, so Jake became my legal guardian. After I turned eighteen we talked about it and decided there was no hurry for me to move out. We were both alone in the world and enjoyed each other's company."

"So you still live together?" I asked.

"No. A few months ago I noticed Jake paying attention to one of the other members of the team—a doctor named Jordan Fairchild. At first I wasn't really sure what I was sensing; Jake and Jordan had been friends for a long time, and she was good friends with my sister. But after a while it became evident that there was something more going on than just friendship. I asked him about it and he insisted they were just friends, but I was definitely picking up more of a lusty vibe."

I laughed. That sounded exactly like something I'd say.

"Jake lives in a large, two-story house next to the tavern, so there was always plenty of room for both of us, but there's an entire floor above the tavern that wasn't being used. I talked Jake into letting me turn the space into an apartment. I want Jake and Jordan to have their shot. I love them both, and Val has been gone for a long time. It's time for Jake to move on, and Jordan is perfect for him. I knew that as long as I was living in his house they'd never get together, so I convinced Jake that I needed my space."

"So you live there alone?"

"No, I live there with Whiskey."

"The whiskey is stored upstairs?" I wondered.

Harmony laughed. "Whiskey is a cat. He was a stray who wandered in during a storm a few years ago and has lived in the tavern ever since. Before I moved in I chatted with Whiskey about sharing the space, and he indicated that he was happy for the company."

Did I mention I love this girl? When I tell people that I chat with Charlie about stuff they usually roll their eyes like I'm crazy, but I had the feeling Harmony would understand completely.

"Isn't living in a tavern kind of noisy?" I asked.

Harmony shrugged. "Not really. It's closed on Sundays and Mondays during the winter and only open from four to ten Tuesdays through Thursdays and four to midnight on Fridays and Saturdays. I work at the tavern, so when it's open I'm downstairs anyway. It's convenient to live there because I only have to go downstairs to go to work. Besides, the tavern serves as the command post during Search and Rescue operations, and I'm usually assigned to man the radio because I don't have specialized skills like the others."

Harmony turned off the highway onto a narrow side road that paralleled a body of water I couldn't make out with all the snow but was pretty sure was the large lake I'd seen on the map.

"Does that lake freeze over in the winter?" I asked.

"No, not completely. There are some smaller fingers that freeze, but the main body of water is really deep, and it doesn't get as cold here as it does in the northern parts of the state. The main problem we have is that at times the smaller bodies of water freeze just enough to entice ice skaters but not enough to safely hold their weight. Thin ice results in at least a couple of rescues every winter."

I looked out the window at the sheet of white. I couldn't see landmarks of any type. It was a good thing Harmony had picked us up; I'm certain Zak and

I would have gotten lost if we'd rented a car and driven to the tavern, as we'd originally planned to do.

"Who all is on the S and R team?" I asked as we crossed a bridge. I was interested to find out who I'd be working with during the next few days.

"Jake is the team leader. As I mentioned, he owns the tavern we use as a command post, so I guess that gives him a sort of proprietary leadership, but he's also better than anyone at wilderness survival. He can ski better than anyone, climb better than anyone, and dive deeper than anyone. And he never seems to run out of energy, no matter how difficult the rescue. Don't repeat this, but if you ask me, he's determined that no one will lose a loved one the way he lost Val, so he goes above and beyond what seems humanly possible at times."

"He sounds like a great guy. I can't wait to meet him."

"He's the best," Harmony confirmed. "He'll be Sitka's official handler, so you'll be working closely together this week."

"I'm looking forward to it."

Harmony turned onto a narrow road that veered away from the lake. She wasn't wrong about the level of darkness that could be experienced during a stormy Alaskan night. As hard as I tried, I couldn't even begin to make out the road in front of us.

"So who else is on the team?" I asked as I tried to distract myself from the fact that Harmony might know the area, but she couldn't see any better than I could.

"Jordan Fairchild is a doctor."

"And this is the team member you think Jake has been lusting after?"

"Exactly. You'll like Jordan. She has this seriousness about her that can come off as standoffish at times, but once you get to know her you'll see that she's really great."

"I look forward to meeting her."

I turned around and laughed as Zak let out a loud snort as he slept.

"Poor guy seems exhausted," Harmony observed.

"Yeah, he really is." I'd looked forward to coming to Alaska, but with everything that had happened, I hoped the training would go quickly so I could get home to my friends. "So other than Jake and Jordan, who else is on the team?" I figured I might as well get a head start on learning everyone's name.

"Dani Matthews owns a helicopter she uses for tours and heliskiing in order to make a living, but she also serves as an air ambulance for the area," Harmony continued. "And of course she's always willing to provide air support for a rescue. We also have a man named Landon Stanford on the team. He's a geologist who's really smart and can help with information relating to snow loads and avalanche potential. He even predicted our last earthquake. He's a fun guy to know but a hard guy to get to know, if you know what I mean."

"Smart and quiet. Got it."

"The last member of the team is a man named Wyatt Forester," Harmony informed me as she pulled onto a main street with shops on both sides. Moosehead certainly was a cute little town. It reminded me quite a lot of Ashton Falls, with its charming shops and small town feel. Many of the buildings were fashioned from logs, as many of the buildings in Ashton Falls were.

"He comes off as being this big playboy, party guy, but if you need someone to be there for you—I mean really be there for you—then he's your guy," Harmony continued. "He's athletic like Jake but not as responsible, and he's smart like Landon but not as serious. I think you'll like him, but let him know right off that you're engaged or he *will* try to hit on you."

I turned and looked at Zak again; he was still snoring softly. "I'm not worried. Zak can be quite formidable when he's not quite so exhausted. So there are six members of the team including you?"

"We're the main six, but there are others who help out when there's a need."

"Sounds like a good crew," I said.

"They're the best. We all work well together and have been best friends since we were kids. It really is an ideal situation."

"So everyone is about the same age?" I wondered.

"No. I'm the baby at twenty-five. Jake is thirty-two and Landon is the oldest at thirty-four. Jake, Jordan, Landon, and Wyatt were friends of Val's when we were growing up. They all treat me like a kid, but that's okay. I like having the feeling of older siblings now that Val's gone."

"And Dani . . . did she grow up here as well?"

"She did, although at twenty-eight, she's younger than the others, so she didn't really start hanging out with us until Jake established the team."

Harmony pulled into a long drive. There was a quaint building that looked like an old Irish inn sitting on the lakeshore that was outlined with colorful Christmas lights. The tree to the left of the door was covered with tiny white lights and there was a mechanical reindeer to the right.

"Is this the tavern?" I asked.

"Yep, this is Neverland. It used to be an inn but was converted into the tavern and grill. It's really quite cozy and charming inside. I think you'll like it."

"And the body of water it sits on?"

"Woodsman's Lake. You can't see much tonight for all the snow, but it's really beautiful when you can see it." Harmony pulled to a complete stop.

I turned and looked at Zak. "Wake up, sleepyhead; we're here."

Zak yawned. "Already?"

"Don't worry; once I drop off Sitka and introduce you around—assuming the others are back from the rescue to be introduced to—I'll take you to the inn."

"Inn?" I asked. "I thought we were staying in a summer house."

"You were until Jake went out to check on the wood supply and found broken pipes. You'll like the inn. It's really comfortable and the* owners are supernice."

"And they'll be okay with Charlie staying with us?"

"Absolutely. The Millers own a dogsled team, so they love and understand dogs. Marty is a really fun guy to talk to. He's lived here for quite a while, so he knows a lot about the area, and Mary is a fantastic cook. I think you'll find it a much superior option to a drafty old summer house."

"And meals are provided?" I asked.

"They are, or if you want a change of pace you can always eat at Neverland in the evenings. Our cook is retired military, and although he can come off like a bit of a curmudgeon at times, he does have a way with a spatula. Other than the specials Serge comes up with, you won't find fine dining at the tavern, but the burgers, soups, and sandwiches are pretty good. And if you want an option for breakfast or lunch, my best friend Chloe owns a coffee shop called Chloe's Corner. She serves breakfast and lunch. She's a really good cook, and her pies and pastries are legendary, so you should make a point to stop by at least once while you're here."

"We will," I promised.

"It looks like the guys are still gone," Harmony observed. "I can make you something to eat if you want to wait a bit."

"I'm starving, so that would be great."

I followed Harmony inside the tavern, which was as warm and inviting as she'd promised. It was still decked out with Christmas decorations, which I imagined would be removed after the New Year. The entire wall that overlooked the lake, which you couldn't actually see at this point due to all the snow, was covered in windows and sliding doors that led out to a large outdoor deck, which again was covered in the white stuff. The floors were wood, the entries arched, and the tables long and wooden, just like you'd find in an old-fashioned tavern. There was a fireplace on one wall with a warm and crackling fire, and the smell coming from the kitchen made me salivate. The only negative I could find in the quaint and cozy room was a moose head prominently displayed on one wall.

"That's Atka," Harmony informed me as Sitka wandered around the room, refamiliarizing himself with his old haunt.

I grimaced. "You named a moose you killed and hung on the wall?"

Harmony laughed. "Of course not. I would never do that, nor would Jake. Atka came with the tavern. He's hung in that spot for over a hundred years. There's a popular legend connected with the moose; would you like to hear it?"

"Maybe while we eat," I suggested hopefully. The tavern really did smell wonderful and I really was starving.

Harmony laughed. "Of course. Serge left a pot of seafood chowder on the stove, which is what you smell, if that sounds good."

"That sounds perfect."

"Zak?" Harmony asked.

Zak had received a text as we arrived, so he'd stayed in the van to return the call while we came inside. He'd be in as soon as he completed his conversation, which sounded a lot like a computer software emergency of some sort, and I knew he'd be hungry as well.

"I'm sure Zak would love a bowl."

"Follow me to the kitchen and we'll stick some homemade bread in the oven to warm too."

Harmony was greeted by a large, multicolored cat who'd been sleeping near the small potbellied stove that stood in one corner of the kitchen. "This is Whiskey," she introduced as she picked the cat up. Charlie, who had been staying close to my side since we'd entered the building, looked cautiously at the cat while Sitka romped over to say hi.

"He's really beautiful. And so big. He looks like a Maine coon."

"I think he is, at least partly. It's hard to know for certain without knowing his background."

Harmony set the cat down on the floor. Sitka took a step back when Whiskey hissed at him.

"Be nice," Harmony admonished the bossy cat.

"You don't get into trouble with the board of health for allowing a cat to live in the tavern?" I asked.

"I'm pretty sure the board doesn't even know where Moosehead, Alaska, is. We're pretty relaxed around here, and Whiskey is popular with the bar's patrons."

"Is the tavern closed tonight?" The building was completely empty even though it was a Saturday night.

"It was open earlier, but between the snow and the rescue Jake decided to hang out the closed sign until we reopen on Tuesday, which will give you time to work with Sitka. We're having our annual New Year's Eve party on Wednesday. You and Zak should plan to come. Most of the town will be here."

"Sounds like fun."

The kitchen was clean and utilitarian. The soup looked as fantastic as it smelled. Harmony gave it a stir and then placed a loaf of homemade bread in the oven to heat.

"So tell me about Atka," I encouraged.

"The legend tells of a group of travelers who came to the area from the east before the town of Moosehead even existed. They intended to make their way to the gulf, where they had a boat waiting to take them to ports to the west, but they became disoriented in a storm and ended up in the mountains to the north. The storm raged for days and the group was forced to dig in against the cold and snow. When the storm passed the group realized they had no idea where they were or how to get back to civilization. The amount of time the group spent on the mountain varies with the telling of the story, but most agree that many of the members were near death and assumed all was lost when a moose showed up at their encampment. The group, figuring they had nothing to lose, followed the moose, which led them to a small settlement that had popped up where Moosehead now stands."

"And they named the moose that led them to safety Atka?" I asked.

"Atka is the Eskimo name for guardian spirit."

"What a great story. Still, I have to wonder how Atka ended up on the wall. They didn't eat him, did they?"

Harmony laughed. "No, they didn't eat him. In fact, the legend says that after the group was delivered to safety the moose headed back toward the north and disappeared, but he came back to the little settlement every summer for a brief period of time. While most of the members of the original group left the area and continued to the gulf, as planned, one small child stayed behind: a boy named Yutu. His parents had died during the journey, so a woodsman who lived in the area took him in. Every summer when the moose returned Yutu would follow him into the mountains, and at the end of the summer the moose would see him safely home. One summer the moose failed to show up, so Yutu went looking for him. He climbed up to the glacier and found the moose had passed during the winter. According to the legend, the moose's body was frozen through, so Yutu took the head as a remembrance. Later, when the tavern was built, Atka was mounted on the wall in a place of honor. Many believe that he looks out for those who find shelter in the tavern."

"Aw, that's actually kind of nice," I said. "Do you believe the legend?"

Harmony shrugged. "It makes a nicer story to the alternative, in which the man who built this tavern killed the moose and mounted its head as nothing more than a trophy."

"Yeah, the legend does make a nicer story. Let's go with that," I agreed.

"Would you like a drink?" Harmony offered. "We have beer, wine, and a full bar, as well as coffee, soft drinks, and juice. Really pretty much anything you could want."

"Maybe coffee for now."

Harmony put on a fresh pot before she wandered over to refill Whiskey's water dish and set out a larger dish for the dogs. I noticed that both dogs were giving the grouchy cat a wide berth. Charlie liked cats, having lived with multiple felines his entire life, but there was something about this tabby, which was almost as big as he was, that seemed to give him pause.

"So what exactly do you do in the tavern?" I asked as I watched Harmony scurry around taking care of random chores.

"Everything. I wait tables, tend bar, help in the kitchen when needed, sweep up, and do the dishes. It's really just Jake, Serge, and me during the winter, so we all pitch in to make it work. During the summer, when the deck is open and we have tourists in the area, we hire part-time staff to help out."

"Is Serge helping with the rescue?" I wondered.

"He's manning the base radio because I had to go pick you up. He didn't want to hang out here by himself, so he went over to Jake's place, where he could man the radio and watch the big-screen TV at the same time. I think I'll go over there to see what's going on if he doesn't come back here in the next few minutes."

"Who's lost?" I asked.

"Two men were separated from a larger group that went up the mountain to ski. They tried to locate the missing men themselves, but when the storm started to roll in and they still hadn't found their friends they notified the sheriff, who called Jake, who rounded up the team. I wouldn't worry. They'll find them. Jake and the team have an excellent track record."

"Have you ever had to give up on a rescue effort before you were able to find someone?" I wondered.

Harmony's smile faded. "Just once. His name was Devon Miles. He was Dani's fiancé and Jake's best friend. He went out on a rescue five years ago and simply disappeared. The team looked and looked, but there wasn't any trace of him. We never did find his body."

Chapter 3

"So it's as awesome as you hoped?" Ellie asked later that evening. I'd called her once Zak and I had been driven to the inn and introduced to Marty and Mary. It was as cozy and inviting as Harmony had promised, and the icing on the cake as far as I was concerned was that the Christmas tree and decorations were still prominently displayed for all to enjoy. I hadn't had a lot of time to really look around, but I did notice quite a few antiques dispersed around the main floor, which gave the inn a look of history and permanence.

"It really is. I think. To be honest, it's all sort of been a blur. It's snowing like crazy and it's dark, so I can't see the scenery, but I've been told it's breathtaking. Maybe I can get some photos tomorrow to e-mail to you."

I looked around the comfortable room Zak and I had been shown to. There was a huge king-size bed, with a feather comforter and warm flannel sheets, into which Zak had promptly climbed and fallen asleep. A fire had been set in the fireplace and the windows in the small seating area looked out over the lake. Or at least I'd been told they did. As I mentioned to Ellie, at this point all I could see was white.

"The carpet in this room is a plush pile that squishes when you walk on it," I informed my best friend. "I've been thinking about getting carpet for Zak's room. The hardwood floor is beautiful but cold even with the throw rugs. This carpet is so soft and warm. It's like walking on a cloud."

Ellie laughed. "Zak's room? I suppose now that you and Zak are engaged you should start referring to the house and the bedroom as *our* house and *our* bedroom."

"Yeah, I guess you're right. It's sort of a weird transition considering he bought the house before I even started dating him. How are you and Levi doing?"

I could hear Ellie shifting around to change position. "Okay. My whole body aches, but Levi seems okay, and it's been nice staying in Casa Zimmerman. I just wish we could enjoy the pool and spa."

"You can stay another time when you both aren't in casts," I promised. "Is Tiffany taking good care of you?"

"Yeah, but we really don't need the help and I think she feels odd waiting on us. She got a call from her mom, who wants her to come for a visit. I told her that she really didn't need to stay to take care of us, but I don't think she'll agree to abandon her post unless you tell her it's okay to do so."

"I'll talk to her," I promised. "Has there been any progress tracking down the man who did this to you?"

"Not really. Levi is furious and is threatening to run his own investigation if Salinger doesn't come up with some answers soon. I know he's made some calls, and he's been on his computer a lot, but so far he's stayed put. I think he wants to be certain I'm taken care of, but I'm not sure how long I can keep him from going out and digging around."

"Digging where?" I asked. "Does he even have any suspects?"

Charlie got up from his spot between Zak and me and wandered down to the bottom of the bed after Zak rolled over and almost squished him.

"I don't know whether he has any leads or not. Ever since Levi and I had our talk on Christmas Eve, he's stopped treating me like a buddy and started treating me like a delicate flower who needs to be protected."

I laughed. "Welcome to girlfriend land. I haven't really had a chance to talk to you since our chat on Christmas Eve. Other than the overprotecting, is everything okay between the two of you?"

Levi and Ellie had traveled a long and painful road in order to get to this point, and I was certain that as much as they both wanted to be with the other, there would be a few hiccups along the way.

"The first night was as magical as I've ever imagined," Ellie shared in a dreamy voice. "I was really scared to bring up our relationship and almost chickened out, but I wanted Levi to stay that night so I plunged ahead. I won't say we've totally worked out all the details of our relationship, but I do know we love each other and we both are committed to making it work."

"So it was a special night?"

"It was the stuff dreams are made of," Ellie confirmed. "And Christmas Day . . . well, let's just say we never did make it to my mom's for dinner. If you'd asked me about our relationship prior to the accident I would have said it was perfect, but I'm not sure how much more coddling I can take."

"You have a broken leg and a bruised arm. I'm sure coddling is in order," I reminded her.

"Maybe, but Levi has a broken arm and it hasn't slowed him down at all. He's barely missed a beat, but every time I even hint that there might be something I want or need he's running around to get it for me."

"A broken arm isn't at all as severe as a broken leg," I reminded her. "He doesn't want you irritating the break, hence the running around getting things for you."

"Maybe, but all this fussing is going to drive me crazy."

I took a deep breath before I continued. "Levi loves you. He was driving when the accident occurred, and even though there was nothing he could have done, if I know Levi, he probably feels responsible for your pain. He needs to try to alleviate that guilt by taking care of you. Let him. He needs it, and you really are supposed to be taking it easy."

Ellie sighed. "Yeah, I guess you're right. I'm just not used to all of this sitting around."

"I know."

"So tell me about the people you've met," Ellie suggested. I could sense she needed a distraction, so even though all I wanted to do was join Zak in the big comfy bed, I decided to play along. "Did Sitka get all settled in?"

"He did," I informed her. "His handler's name is Jake and he owns the tavern and grill where everyone hangs out."

"And Sitka seemed happy to see him?"

"He was ecstatic to see him," I confirmed.

"Good. I'm happy he's in a good placement. I want him to be happy."

"Jake is great," I reassured her. "I'm sure you would like him if you met him. He has this way about him that can best be described as quiet confidence. There was a rescue going on tonight, and it was obvious to me that Jake was a take-charge-and-get-it-handled type of guy."

"You sound impressed."

"I am."

"You aren't crushing on him, are you?" Ellie teased. I could almost picture her impish grin as she said it.

"No, I'm not crushing on him. I have Zak. Who I love. But Jake is a remarkable guy."

"And a babe?"

"Oh, yeah. Tall and fit, with blue eyes and dark brown hair."

"Sounds like Levi," Ellie observed.

"Actually, he sort of reminds me of Levi, minus the boyish charm. In this group it's Wyatt who has the boyish charm, but he has blond hair and sort of looks like a surfer."

"Wyatt is a nice name. I always thought if I had a baby and he was a boy I might want to name him Wyatt."

"It *is* a nice name, and Wyatt seems like a really nice guy. There's also another guy named Landon, who's a scientist of some sort. He's pretty quiet, but Harmony assured me that he's very smart."

"Harmony?"

I climbed into the bed, leaned back against the wall behind me, and pulled the covers over my legs. Even with the fire, it was getting a bit nippy in the room.

"Harmony is one of the girls on the team," I answered. "She lives in an apartment over the bar with a huge cat named Whiskey. I think you'd really like her. She kind of reminds me of you. So sweet you just want to hug her all the time."

Ellie laughed. "You didn't happen to have a drink when you were at the bar, did you?"

"Maybe one," I admitted. I suppressed a yawn. "I really should say good night. It's late and I've had a long day. I'll call you tomorrow."

"Okay. Can you talk to Tiffany?" Ellie reminded me.

"Is she still awake?"

"Yeah. Hang on and I'll get her."

I heard Ellie yell for Tiffany to come to the phone. Poor Ellie. It really would be a drag not to be fully mobile. I hoped that forced confinement so early in the new relationship she was building with Levi wouldn't lead to a premature end. I still remembered the time when Levi, Ellie, and I were eight and all came down with chickenpox at the same time. We all had to stay out of school, and both Levi and Ellie's parents had jobs that were difficult to get out of, so my grandma kept the three of us at her house during the day. I loved the company, but by the end of the week Levi and Ellie were at each other's throats.

After I spoke to Tiffany, assuring her that it was perfectly okay for her to go visit her mom for a few days, I got up and headed down to the kitchen for a glass of milk. When we first met the Millers, who lived in a double suite on the top floor, they'd informed us that we should feel free to use any of the common areas, including the kitchen. As tired as I was, I still felt overly stimulated, and a glass of milk warmed in the microwave usually helped put me to sleep.

The inn had four stories, each of the top three housing four bedroom suites with their own bath and amenities similar to ours. On the ground floor were the kitchen and dining area, as well as a common sitting area that featured several overstuffed sofas as well as a game table with a jigsaw puzzle laid out on it and a large river-rock fireplace. There were battery-operated candles set strategically around the room, and Mary had left the tree lights on, giving the room a soft glow.

I poured a glass of milk and decided to wander around, exploring the first floor as I drank it. It seemed that Charlie, who was sleeping with Zak, was the only animal in residence. While the Millers did own a sled-dog team, I found they were housed in a kennel at the back of the property. I must have shown a look of disapproval when Mary mentioned that the dogs rarely came inside because she quickly explained that the dogs actually preferred the cooler interior of the kennel to the warm temperature of the inn. I supposed that made sense; huskies were bred to have thick coats with heavy undercoats to protect them from the cold.

I looked out the window toward the area where Mary had indicated the kennel was located. It was still snowing hard enough that I couldn't make out the building, but I was quite interested to learn more about the team and the specialized training they received. I was about to return to my room when I noticed that the light was on under the door of the room Mary had pointed out as the library and reading room. I knocked gently and slowly opened the door when there was no answer.

"Hello," I called softly so as not to wake the people sleeping on the upper floors. When there was no answer I continued on inside. There was a man I hadn't met asleep in one of the chairs. I didn't want to disturb him, so I turned to leave just as I noticed something that sent my heart plunging toward my stomach.

"Not again," I whispered as I checked the man's pulse to determine what I already knew to be true. The Moosehead Inn had one guest who might have checked in but wouldn't be checking out.

Chapter 4

Sunday, December 28

The sheriff's office in Moosehead consisted of one person, a portly man who went by the name of Orson Kingman. Orson also owned the general store, where he kept an office in which he conducted interviews. Moosehead wasn't large enough for its own jail, so anyone who might be charged with a crime was transported to the main office in the larger city nearby. If someone needed to be temporarily locked up until transport could be arranged, the empty storage room at the back of the building was utilized. Suffice it to say that Moosehead was a town with very little crime.

"This has to be the strangest postmurder interview I've ever witnessed," I whispered to Zak.

After I'd found the body I'd woken up Zak and Marty and Mary Miller. Mary had fainted while Marty called Orson, who promised to be by as soon as he could dig his truck out of the snow. I took an extra blanket from our room and placed it over the victim, who appeared to have been strangled from behind.

Once Orson arrived Mary offered him some of her bundt cake, which he promptly accepted. Orson, Marty, and Mary had been sitting at the dining table drinking coffee, eating cake, and chatting about the storm ever since.

"Maybe Orson likes to ease into the harder questions," Zak, who was sitting on the sofa next to Charlie and me, whispered back.

"The man is on his second piece of cake," I said. "And what's up with those pants?"

The pants I was referring to were actually pajama bottoms. It looked as if the man had rolled out of bed, pulled on some boots and a jacket, and then gone straight out to take care of the snowdrift around his truck without even bothering to change into actual clothing. I couldn't help but giggle as I tried to imagine Sheriff Salinger showing up at a murder scene dressed in nothing but pajamas, boots, and a jacket.

"I'm not sure it's appropriate to be sitting here laughing," Zak reminded me as both Marty and Mary stopped talking to turn and stare at me.

"I can't help it," I whispered. "The man has on pa-ja-mas." I drew out the word for emphasis.

"This is a small town in the middle of nowhere," Zak pointed out. "Maybe the way of life here is a bit more relaxed than we're used to."

"Pa-ja-mas," I said again.

This time I noticed Zak physically suppressing his own chuckle. I love his little half smiles when he tries not to grin but can't quite help it.

"Based on the rate with which he's conducting this interview, maybe he figured he'd be spending the night." Zak smirked.

I put my hand over my mouth to hide my grin. "Seriously. The man is as slow as molasses. He knows the killer has to be someone sleeping upstairs, so why doesn't he just wake everyone up and get on with it?"

"Maybe he's waiting for them to wake up so he can interview them one at a time." Zak yawned.

"Yeah, I guess." I put my head on Zak's shoulder and tried not to show my impatience. It seemed pretty cut-and-dried to me. The inn had been locked with dead bolts from the inside when the murder occurred. It was the middle of winter, so all of the exterior windows were closed and winterized. Marty had reported that he's gone from room to room on the first floor, straightening up and turning off lights, before going up for the night to the rooms he shared with Mary. There hadn't been anyone in the study at the time he'd made his final rounds, so the victim had to have entered the study after Marty locked up.

Mary had reported that she'd verified that everyone was on-site before locking the exterior doors. It seemed that Zak and I had been the last to arrive, which hadn't been until close to eleven by the time we'd finished chatting with the S&R team, who had arrived back at the tavern while we were eating the soup Harmony had reheated for us. Everyone else had gone up for the night already, and Zak and I had chatted with Marty and Mary for a few minutes and then gone up to our own room, where Zak had promptly fallen asleep and I had called Ellie, who I'd suspected would be waiting to hear from me. It had been just after midnight when I'd come downstairs and found the body.

I looked at the clock, which showed me that it was now four o'clock in the morning. I never had been to bed and I realized that I most likely wouldn't have the chance to do so before I was scheduled to meet up with Jake at eleven to begin our training. At least the warmth from the fire was nice, and Zak's shoulder made a nice pillow. Maybe I'd just rest my eyes while I waited for Orson to finish his second piece of cake.

"Zoe, wake up." Zak nudged me.

I looked at the clock again; it was seven-fifteen.

"The first guests have come downstairs," he informed me.

I knew there had been fourteen people in the inn when the doors had been locked the previous evening: Zak and me, inn owners Marty and Mary, the victim—who, it turned out, was a traveling salesman from out of the area who'd checked in under the name Colin Michaels—and nine others. The first to come downstairs was Grover Wood, a visiting geologist, who had been staying at the inn for several weeks and planned to be there through January at a minimum. His reservation was open-ended because the duration of his stay depended primarily on the outcome of his research.

After pouring the man a cup of coffee, Mary retired to the kitchen and Marty went outdoors to gather additional wood for the multiple fireplaces the inn featured. Zak and I went upstairs to shower and change, giving Orson a chance to speak to Grover in private.

"Talk about a long night." Zak rotated his neck to work out the kink that must have formed as he slept sitting up. "Orson never did interview us; we should have just gone to bed."

"Yeah; why didn't he interview us?" I wondered. "I found the body after everyone else was fast asleep. I could have killed the man and then alerted everyone that he'd been murdered in order to cover up my guilt."

"You're too short," Zak pointed out.

"Too short?"

"The man was strangled from behind. I'm going to go out on a limb and say that he fell asleep in the chair because he was facing the door and would have seen his attacker had he been awake. The killer used some sort of a tie to kill Colin, which he or she wrapped around his neck and then pulled up on. I'm guessing the attacker was at least five foot ten inches. Maybe taller."

"So it could have been you."

"Yes, I suppose it could have. If I were Orson I'd be looking for the murder weapon before the killer has a chance to dispose of it."

"What if the person who choked Colin didn't use a tie? What if he or she used his or her hands?"

"No," Zak seemed certain, "I'm confident the killer used a binding device of some type. I'd say something thick, without sharp edges, like a necktie or the sash to a robe or wraparound sweater."

"How did you figure out all that?" I asked.

"I got a look at the body when we were waiting for Orson. The neck didn't show any marks that would come from fingers, nor did it show the kind of deep wound that would come from using a small diameter tool such as a drape cord or power cord to do the choking. I guess we'll have to wait to know for sure what was used, but I'm going to stick with a necktie for now."

"Wow, look at you doing the Sherlock thing." I wrapped my arms around Zak's neck. There's nothing hotter than a smart man dressed in nothing but a rose-colored towel.

When I came back downstairs Harmony was in the living room. She hurried over and wrapped me in a tight hug. "You poor thing," she said. "You must be traumatized."

I hesitated to tell my new friend that I found dead bodies on almost a monthly basis, so I mumbled something about being sorry for the man and his family and hoping the killer would be found.

"What are you doing here?" I asked.

"I came to fetch the skiers."

I looked outside and saw the snow had stalled to a few flurries.

"The National Weather Service is calling for a break in the storm until after sunset, so Dani decided to go ahead with the heliskiing tour that was scheduled," Harmony informed me. "They missed yesterday due to the weather, so she wanted to strike while she could."

"And you work for Dani?" I asked.

"No, but I do help her out at times. She wanted to go on ahead to the airport to do an inspection of the copter after last night's rescue. I knew she was on a tight timeline, so I volunteered to come pick up the skiers and deliver them to the airport."

"Mary mentioned something about having skiers on the third floor. Who are you supposed to pick up?"

Harmony looked down at her list. "Jerid Richardson, for one. He's been here for over a week and has gone out every day Dani has had a tour. She told me that he's a really good snowboarder. Like Olympics kind of good. I guess he's staying until after the New Year because Dani mentioned she was going to ask him to accompany her to Jake's New Year's Eve party."

I made a mental note to look into this Jerid Richardson. I'd overheard one of the others saying that the victim, Colin Michaels, had been complaining about the amount of noise made by Jerid, who was staying in the room above him. Apparently, the inn had been booked since the first of December, so there was no way to move either of the men. Colin had bragged to anyone who would listen that he was going to take matters into his own hands if Jerid didn't keep it down. Could Jerid and Colin have gotten into a skirmish, with Colin ending up the victim rather than the victor? Jerid was at least six feet tall and he had been at the inn for over a week, so he knew his way around.

"Who else?" I asked.

"Turner Hawthorn. He also got here over a week ago and has been skiing at every opportunity. According to Dani, he skis okay but never says much. Also going today will be first-timers Barry and Stella Ward, a couple on their honeymoon, and Liza Aldren."

"*The* Liza Aldren?" I asked.

"The one and only," Harmony confirmed.

Liza Aldren was a six-foot-tall, dark-haired beauty, one of the top models in the world. I couldn't imagine what she would be doing in a town like Moosehead. According to the tabloids, she spent most of her time in five-star hotels and luxury resorts.

"Do you ski?" Harmony asked.

"Since before I could walk," I exaggerated.

"You should go up with Dani one day if she has room. Heliskiing down an ungroomed mountain is a rush like you've never had."

"I'd like that. How many skiers can Dani take at once?"

"Five passengers, if they all have gear. She's booked for the next couple of days, but if you're going to be here after New Year's most of the tourists will have gone home."

"I remember Mary mentioning that she'd be glad when the inn was back to housing the longer-term customers."

"Yeah; it's been a crazy month, I'm sure." Harmony smiled. "Once I get this group delivered I'll come back by and take you to Neverland to meet up with Jake and Sitka."

"I'll be ready."

I tried to remember what Mary had told me about the long-term guests. There was a woman who basically lived on the top floor, in the unit on the far right, which would be 3D. Marty and Mary lived in the double unit 3A/B, and Zak and I were currently staying in unit 3C. The woman in 3D was some kind of heiress who traveled quite extensively, but when she wasn't traveling she called the Moosehead Inn home.

"Can I help you with something?" a short, stick-thin man who looked to be about seventy asked me.

I guess I must have looked confused as I stood in the middle of the room, staring into space, while I tried to remember what I knew about the inn's residents.

"No." I smiled. "I must have been daydreaming. My name is Zoe Donovan. I just arrived last night."

"So you're the little lady who found the body. I must say, you don't look all that upset." The man looked at me suspiciously. "Most of the women I know would have taken to their bed after a thing like that."

"My dog Charlie is a therapy dog, so I spend a lot of time working in the hospital," I offered as a simple yet believable excuse. "I don't shock easily."

"I see." The man hadn't softened his glare. "Where exactly is this dog of yours?"

"Upstairs, with my fiancé, Zak. I'm sorry; I don't think I caught your name."

"Bart Lansing. I'm a retired history professor, staying at the inn for the winter while I write my memoirs."

"This seems like a good place to find some peace and quiet in order to write," I commented as I looked around the isolated yet cozy retreat. "I remember Marty mentioning a mystery writer was staying here as well."

"Drake Rutherford," Bart confirmed. "He writes thrillers."

"I haven't heard of him, but Marty seems to think highly of him."

"You might not have heard of Drake Rutherford because he writes under the name D. R. Ford."

"D. R. Ford? I've heard of him *and* read his work. He's really good."

"Yes." The man looked me up and down. "He is. What did you say your name was again?"

"Zoe. Zoe Donovan."

He continued to study me. "I'm sorry to seem so suspicious, but Marty and Mary are good folk, and I don't want to see them get hurt."

"That's the last thing I'd want to see happen as well," I assured the man, who was almost as short as I was and so most likely not the killer. "I'm actually in the area to deliver a new search and rescue dog to the team."

"You know Jake and the gang?" He smiled for the first time.

"I met them briefly last night. We plan to work together this afternoon."

"Well then, okay." The man finally seemed satisfied that I wasn't a serial killer or some other sort of deranged murderer. "I'm heading in for breakfast; would you care to accompany me?" He held out his elbow in a chivalrous fashion.

"I'd be honored."

Chapter 5

Jake and Sitka were waiting for us when Harmony, Zak, Charlie, and I arrived at the tavern. I found I was regretting the large brunch I'd eaten at the inn when I noticed the snowshoes lined up by the bar. Not that a good workout wasn't exactly what I needed, but after the long night I'd had, the large meal had made me sleepy.

"Do you snowshoe?" Jake asked as Charlie trotted over to greet Sitka, who'd wagged his entire body but stayed dutifully at Jake's side when we'd walked into the building.

"I do," I confirmed. "Can Charlie stay here with you?" I asked Harmony.

"Absolutely."

I noticed Whiskey eyeing Charlie from his perch on top of the bar. I hoped the big cat wouldn't pick on my little dog.

"You want to come?" I asked Zak, who looked longingly at the comfy chair in front of the fire.

"Sure, if you'd like."

"Actually," I decided to take pity on my poor exhausted fiancé, "it might be better if Jake and I took Sitka out alone the first time."

"If you think that's best." Zak looked relieved.

Poor Zak. He really did look beat. I hoped he wasn't coming down with something. He'd been running full steam ahead for days, and I knew that eventually his body would have no choice but to shut down. At least I'd been able to sleep in on the 26th, which had allowed me to catch up from our Christmas marathon of activity.

After strapping on the snowshoes Jake provided, he and I headed out into the crisp yet frigid air. The snow had stopped temporarily, but with the clear sky came colder temperatures than I'd experienced thus far. For the next several hours Jake and I hiked through the deep snow as I demonstrated the commands Peter had taught Sitka. Jake had worked with S&R dogs for years and so wasn't new to the methods used, but each trainer, it seemed, took a slightly different approach to the task. In a way, introducing Jake to Sitka's routine was a lot like having a salesman show you where the controls for the headlights and windshield wipers were on a new car. Every car had them, but they each seemed to have a slightly different way of obtaining the desired result.

"It's so beautiful out here," I commented as we stopped for a breather.

"If there's one thing you can say for Alaska it's that we have plenty of untrodden land and clean air and water to go around."

"Don't get me wrong: Ashton Falls is beautiful, but this is really extraordinary." I looked around at the tall, snow-covered mountains and the vast expanse of barren land. "Do you get a good view of the Northern Lights from here?"

"We get a glimpse at times, although the best viewing is farther north. If you really want to get a good look you should plan to visit Fairbanks during either the spring or the fall equinox."

"I just might do that. I'd love to see them. I imagine they're really spectacular."

"They're pretty awesome," Jake agreed. "I had the good fortune to be driving the Alaskan Highway toward Prudhoe Bay a couple of years ago on a perfectly clear night when the lights were at their brightest. I just pulled over and let the beauty of the moment wrap itself around me. It was really magical."

"I can imagine. I'll definitely make plans to return to the area when the lights are most likely to be seen, although standing around on a cold winter's night waiting for them to appear might not be all it's cracked up to be."

Jake laughed. "Yeah, you're most likely to happen upon them during the long winter nights, but it's also possible to see them during times of the year when it isn't quite as cold."

"I'd like to come back when it's warmer. Do you have a lot of wildlife in the summer?"

"We do." Jake's eyes lit up as he spoke about the land it was obvious he loved. "Both black and brown bears here in the south and polar bears farther north. And we have moose, wolves, elk, and caribou, among other animals. If you spend as much time away from the populated areas as I do, you can experience a wilderness few ever see."

"It sounds wonderful."

Although we have coyotes and foxes in Ashton Falls, I'd never seen a wolf in the wild, and I realized that must be a truly awesome experience. "We have black bears that can prove to be quite a nuisance at times, but we don't have the variety you do. I'd love to come back during the summer."

"You should, though the town is a lot busier then, so you'd need to plan ahead. The inn fills up from June through Labor Day, but now that I've met you,

I'd be happy to have you and Zak stay in one of my spare rooms."

"You have spare rooms?" I wondered why he hadn't just let us stay with him on this visit. It certainly would have been more convenient.

"Three of them, but I'm pretty particular about who I share my space with. I hadn't yet met you and there was a room at the inn, so I figured that would be the safer choice."

"In case I was a whistler," I teased.

"Yeah, something like that." Jake grinned.

I had to laugh. At least the man was honest.

"I guess the tavern must be busy during the summer as well."

"It is. In fact, the whole team is pretty busy, which makes it hard when there's a rescue."

"I remember Harmony saying that Jordan is a doctor and Landon a geologist, but I can't seem to recall what Wyatt does."

"In the winter not a lot, but during the summer Dani and Wyatt team up to do hiking tours. Basically, she drops the group off at the top of that glacier over there," Jake pointed to a tall mountain in the distance, "and then Wyatt leads the group back down. It takes several days to a week to get back to the bottom, depending on the route chosen."

"It sounds like fun."

"It is. If you come back you should join one of the groups."

I looked down at Sitka, who watched Jake as he spoke. "I've noticed that Sitka pays total attention to you," I commented. "He walks right next to you and looks at you with absolute concentration. And the entire time we've been standing here he's been completely focused on everything you do and say."

Jake bent over and scratched Sitka behind the ears. "Harmony and I raised him after Jordan and I rescued him. He's pretty bonded to all of us."

"Harmony told me that the two of you raised him as a puppy, but she didn't mention that you'd rescued him."

Sitka put a paw on Jake's leg, as if to say that he appreciated the scratch.

"Jordan and I were cross-country skiing just after Thanksgiving last year. The winter got off to a slower start than this one, so, although there was snow on the ground, there wasn't as much as there is now. We were just about to head back when we heard a strange noise that seemed to be coming from behind a rock outcropping near where we'd stopped to rest. Luckily, we decided to check it out and found Sitka. He was ten or twelve weeks old at the time. We had no idea how long he'd been there or even how he got there because he was pretty far away from town. Jordan zipped him into her backpack for the trip down the mountain and Harmony and I decided to take him in and raise him. Initially, we only planned on him being a pet, but when we noticed how focused he was on everything we said we realized he could make a good rescue dog. Denali, the dog we'd been working with for the past six years, was about ready to hang up her vest and we knew we'd need another dog, so I called Peter to ask about having him trained."

"You know Peter?" I asked.

"Not at the time. I got his name from a friend who had a police dog trained by him. Sitka and I went for a visit and I was impressed by his facility and his credentials, so I decided to leave Sitka with him. The plan was to bring him back in the spring, but Denali was injured in a rescue a few weeks ago, so Peter agreed to move up the timeline. We really depend on having an avalanche dog in the winter with all these tall mountains and sheer drop-offs, but we knew it was time to retire Denali."

"I haven't noticed another dog. Do you still have Denali?"

"He was placed with Jordan's sister and her family and seems very happy. I would have kept him myself, but it doesn't usually work out all that well to have two male dogs in the house. We should probably start to head back. It'll be dark soon."

I looked at the sun, which was beginning its descent although it was only early afternoon. "Yeah, that sounds like a good idea."

The hike back down the mountain was a lot easier than the one up and only took a fraction of the time. We were almost back to the tavern when Sitka began digging in the snow.

"What's that crazy dog doing?" Jake asked.

"I'm not sure."

I walked over to where the dog had dug a deep hole and then lay down beside it. I looked into the hole and gasped. At the bottom was a yellow ski hat attached to a very frozen face.

Jake looked over my shoulder. "Get the others," he commanded me.

I hurried back to the tavern and informed those who had gathered that Sitka had located his first body on his very first day and everyone's help was needed.

The tavern was closed on Sundays, so the only occupants of the cozy building were the S&R members who had come by at the end of the day to hang out. When I returned alone with my announcement everyone, including Zak, headed out. I decided to wait in the tavern so as not to leave Charlie alone with Harmony's giant cat, who was eyeing him like a tasty midafternoon treat.

"So you live here?" I asked the cat, who had wandered over to the sofa in front of the fireplace where I was waiting for the others.

The cat jumped up onto the sofa and climbed into my lap. Charlie, who was lying at my feet, glanced at us before falling back to sleep.

"It seemed like Jake was really upset about the man in the snow," I informed the cat. "If I had to guess, I'd say he knew him."

Whiskey jumped off my lap and trotted across the room to jump up onto the fireplace mantel, knocking off a framed photograph. I frowned at him before getting up to retrieve the picture, which was of a group of ten people. The photo looked to be several years old at least; I recognized Harmony, who looked like a teenager. Standing next to her was a woman several years older than she was who was standing next to Jake. After studying the photo I realized all six members of the S&R team were there, as well as an additional woman and three other men. One of the men, who stood next to Wyatt, looked eerily like the man I'd seen in the snow.

I turned as someone came into the room through the kitchen. It was Harmony, who was taking off her gloves. Her long dark hair tumbled around her shoulders as she removed her ski cap.

"Did you know the man in the snow?" I asked.

She frowned and looked at me. "His name is—or I guess I should say was—Gary Peterman. He was a friend of Devon's."

I remembered that Devon was Dani's fiancé, who had gone missing during a rescue and never returned.

"Gary moved away after Devon disappeared. No one has seen or heard from him in five years," Harmony continued.

My Zodar launched into full alert. First the murder at the inn and now this? They had to be connected in some way.

"Was Gary part of the team?" I asked.

"No. Why do you ask?"

I held up the photo Whiskey had pushed to the floor.

Harmony crossed the room and looked at it. "This was taken eight years ago. I was just sixteen and Val was still alive. That's her." Harmony pointed to the woman standing between her and Jake.

I continued to look at the photo as Harmony began to point to the people standing in the photo from left to right.

"That's me, Val, Jake, Jordan, Landon, Dani, Devon, Gary, Wyatt, and Walter. The photo was taken at a summer BBQ."

Harmony, Jake, Jordan, Dani, Wyatt, and Landon were all on the S&R team. Val was Jake's wife and Harmony's sister and Devon was Dani's fiancé. Both had been on the team before they died. Gary was Devon's friend, so I assumed he knew the others as well. "Who's Walter?" I asked.

"Walter was a friend of Jake's who was in town for the summer."

"The man who died at the Inn: Colin Michaels. Had you ever met him?" I asked.

"The name isn't familiar."

"And the man in the snow—Gary. How long would you say he'd been dead?"

Harmony shrugged. "Jordan thinks less than a day. She'll know more once they get him to the hospital."

"Is there a hospital in Moosehead?" I asked.

"No, just the clinic Jordan runs. Dani is taking her and the body to the city. The others will be back shortly. I came on ahead to put on some coffee and heat up some soup."

I followed Harmony into the kitchen, where she began rummaging through the refrigerator. "Were any of the team members close to Gary?" I asked as Whiskey jumped up onto the counter to watch.

"Honestly, no. The only reason he was at the BBQ where the photo was taken was because Devon invited him. He was an odd sort. Secretive. Dani didn't like him and was working on talking Devon into parting company with him. She said many times that she didn't trust him. When he left the area we were all glad to see him go."

"Any idea what he might have been doing here now?"

"Not a one. He didn't have family in Moosehead. I'm not even sure how Devon got hooked up with him in the first place. I suppose Dani might know."

"Was Devon from Moosehead originally?" I wondered.

"No," Harmony answered as she began to assemble a salad. She paused what she was doing and frowned. "I'm not sure where Dani met him. I know she introduced him to the rest of the group not long before this photo was taken. They were just friends at first, but Devon wasn't only crazy smart but a pretty good athlete, so the team welcomed him into their inner circle. Unlike Gary, he really fit in. I wasn't actually a member of the team at the point when the photo was taken because I was so young, and my sister didn't want to see me put into dangerous situations. When Devon joined there were seven of them, including Val."

"So Val was an original member of the team?"

"She was, along with Jake, Landon, and Jordan, although Jordan was in college when the group first formed, so she wasn't around much at that point. Landon had just graduated college; neither Jake nor Val ever went. Eventually, Dani and Wyatt joined. There were just the six of them for quite a while, before Dani brought Devon into the group. When Val died they were back to six, and then I turned eighteen and joined, bringing us back to seven. When Devon went missing we were back to six and have stayed that way ever since."

"When did Jordan move back to the area full-time?" I wondered.

"Seven years ago, just after Val died. She'd just completed her residency and decided the big cities in Alaska had plenty of doctors and Moosehead really could use one, so she moved home and opened the clinic."

"Did Moosehead have a doctor at all before she moved home?" I was curious about living in such a small and isolated town.

"Sort of." Harmony cut a loaf of bread in half and buttered both sides before sliding it into the oven.

"We had a guy who worked out of his house who was okay with simple things, but he was getting on in years, and the town was pretty concerned about what we'd do if he moved away or died."

Ashton Falls was a small town by most standards, but we did have luxuries like a public library and sufficient medical care. I could see Harmony loved her town as much as I loved mine, but I wasn't sure how I'd feel about living in an area that was *so* isolated. On the other hand, the people who called Moosehead home seemed dedicated to the place, and that said a lot in my book.

"It's really great that Jordan decided to come home and take care of her town," I commented. "I'm sure she could have made a lot more money working in a large hospital."

"Financially, she gave up a lot to return home. She was at the top of her class and was offered some really spectacular jobs when she graduated. Everyone was very grateful when she announced that she was coming home to practice. She really is an exceptional person, and I'm proud to have her for a friend."

"It seems like everyone on the team is really exceptional," I observed.

"They really are. I was soooo happy when I was finally old enough to work with these awesome people."

"So Jake let you join the team when you became an adult," I clarified.

"Sort of." Harmony laughed. "I got a jacket and underwent rescue training, but Jake still won't let me go on the really dangerous missions. He treats me like a kid even though I'm twenty-five."

"But you don't mind," I guessed.

Harmony smiled. "Not really. I kind of like Jake looking out for me."

I decided to help Harmony serve the food as the others began filing back in. It seemed a little odd to me that the group wasn't more upset about losing someone they knew, but if this Gary wasn't really liked or trusted . . .

"Something smells good." Zak kissed me on the cheek when he wandered in through the side door.

"Salmon chowder. It looks wonderful. Harmony made a salad, heated some bread, and grilled some crab cakes as well."

"Can I help?" Zak asked.

I looked at Harmony.

"No, everything's ready," Harmony answered. "Did Dani and Jordan head out to the hospital?"

"Yeah, and Jake went with them. Landon and Wyatt are right behind me with Sitka. They seem pretty excited about something they found in the dead man's pocket."

"Oh, and what was that?" Harmony asked as she shooed Whiskey off the counter.

"A photograph of the man in the snow talking to another man who I understand was Dani's fiancé, Devon."

Harmony looked up from transferring the hot bread to a basket. "They were friends, so I imagine there would be photos of the men together, but it does seem odd that Gary would be carrying around a photo of the two of them all these years after Devon died."

"The photo was date-stamped. It was taken two weeks ago," Zak informed us.

Harmony turned pale. "But how?"

"That's exactly what Dani and Jake want to know."

Chapter 6

"So the man in the snow has a photo taken two weeks ago of him with a man who disappeared five years ago?" Ellie asked later that evening, when I called to check up on her and Levi. Zak was at the desk in the sitting area, working on his computer, trying to deal with the needs of the client who had called on the night we arrived, Charlie asleep at his feet.

"That about sums it up."

"I don't know how you do it, but you always stumble into the best mysteries. Your case is a lot more interesting than ours."

"How is yours going?" I asked.

"Slowly." Ellie sighed. "Levi tried to talk to Sheriff Salinger, but Salinger absolutely refuses to discuss the case with him. I guess the goodwill you've managed to create with the man doesn't transfer to us."

"Yeah, Salinger is tricky," I acknowledged. "It's taken me a long time to gain his trust, and even with all the cases I solved for him, he still needs to be wooed. I'd be willing to bet Levi went in demanding rather than wooing."

"Yeah, you're probably right. Levi is pretty agitated about the whole thing. I remembered where I'd seen the man, though. It'd been nagging at me ever since the accident happened. He was in the hardware store on Christmas Eve. I'd stopped in to pick up something for my mom and saw a man wandering up and down the aisles. I thought it was odd because he didn't seem to be looking at the shelves. He was walking up one aisle and down the next in a very methodical manner."

"Do you think he was just killing time while he waited for someone?" I asked as I curled my legs up under my body. I was sitting on the bed with my back resting against the headboard. I have to say I'm really loving the feather comforter that tops the warm flannel sheets.

"Maybe. He didn't seem to be shopping as far as I could tell. He didn't have a basket and he wasn't carrying anything. The store was closed today, so Levi's going to go speak to the employees tomorrow. In the meantime, he's been checking with local lodging facilities. If the man was in town on the twenty-fourth and the fire was started on the twenty-sixth, he has to have been staying somewhere."

"That sounds like a good idea. Tracking down someone with a large black truck shouldn't be too hard."

"That's what Levi thinks, but so far he hasn't had any luck."

I glanced out the window. It was snowing again, and it looked like we might not get another break for a couple of days. "So how are you feeling?"

"Okay," Ellie answered. "My leg aches a bit, and I really hate not being able to get around. My arm is doing okay, though, so between Levi and me, we're one complete person." She laughed. "I can open jars and Levi can walk around to fetch things."

"I guess it's good you broke different body parts," I teased.

"Yeah, I guess so. Levi has been really great. He's a little cranky, but I can tell he's trying to keep things upbeat for me. Don't get me wrong: I wish this whole thing never happened and Levi and I were with you in Alaska as we'd planned, but I will say that our forced dependence on each other has served as a bonding situation."

"You've been best friends for twenty years," I pointed out. "I'd say you were already bonded."

"I know, but I'm talking about couple bonding. Being vulnerable and allowing yourself to really depend on the other person. After so many months of dreaming about how Levi and I might be as a couple, partial incapacitation wasn't my choice, but I've decided to look on the bright side and accept this experience as a gift and not a curse."

"That's a good attitude."

I looked toward the window again when the dogs in the kennel started barking. Maybe it was feeding time. I'd seen Marty take the team out for a run earlier in the day.

"Yeah, I guess, although at times it's easier to verbalize than to really feel, if you know what I mean. And it really has been fun staying in your house. Levi and I have made good use of Zak's home theater, as well as his wine cellar."

"Yeah, the wine cellar is nice, and Zak does have a good collection of movies."

"The movies have been a welcome distraction and the animals all seem to like watching too."

"How are Bella, Marlow, and Spade doing?" I asked.

"They're fine. Neither cat is thrilled with the puppy antics we have going on with Shep and Karloff, but they seem to be hanging in okay. Spade likes to hang out in Zak's office and watch the fish and Marlow has been sitting on the landing at the top of the stairs, hissing at the dogs. Bella plays with the other dogs for a while, but she doesn't quite have the never-ending energy of the younger two. I actually found Bella curled up with Spade in Zak's office this morning."

I laughed. Normally Spade doesn't want anything to do with Bella, but I guess it's true what they say about finding common ground in a common enemy.

"Is Buck back in town?" I wondered.

"I heard he is, but I haven't talked to him. Levi spoke to Ethan, who told him that Buck was pretty mad about the whole thing. Not that I blame him. I'm sure this fire is going to set him back a few dollars, even if most of the wood was left undamaged."

I folded a piece of gum into my mouth. The bread Harmony had made had been delicious but garlicky, and the last thing I wanted was garlicky breath when Zak finally finished the work he'd been totally focused on.

"I wonder if the man in the black truck is from Buck's past," I mused. "His incarcerated past, to be exact."

"I don't know. Maybe. I guess that makes as much sense as anything. By the way, your grandpa and Hazel stopped by to see how we were doing today."

"That was nice of them."

"Yeah. It seems like they're really turning into a couple," Ellie observed.

"I think they are. Hazel even has Pappy volunteering at the library a couple of days a week."

"Hazel mentioned that. She also mentioned that some of the members of the events committee were thinking about trying to do some sort of St. Patrick's Day fund-raiser."

I groaned. "Really? March is one of the few months when we don't have a lot going on."

"It seems the whole idea started with Hazel mentioning to Willa that she was thinking about doing a corned beef and cabbage dinner as a fund-raiser for the library. Willa of course took it a step further and suggested that they come up with an idea to turn the dinner into a weekend event that might get some of the tourists from the valley to come up the mountain and spend some of their hard-earned dollars."

Willa was the chairperson for the Ashton Falls Events Committee and was constantly on the lookout for fund-raising activities.

"Has the committee met?" I asked. We usually meet on Tuesdays.

"No, not yet. Hazel brought it up to me because she hoped I had a good corned beef and cabbage recipe. Once we started chatting about the idea she shared the conversation she'd had with Willa. I don't think the committee is meeting this week, so I guess it will come up on the seventh."

"Not that I don't support the fund-raising efforts the committee engages in, but we have the Sweetheart Dance in February and the Easter event in April. It would be nice to have March off."

"I guess you can make your case at the meeting. Hang on."

I could hear Ellie talking to someone in the background.

"Levi wants to talk to you," she informed me when she came back on the line. "Call me tomorrow when you get a chance and let me know how your mystery is developing."

"I will."

I barely had a chance to take a breath before Levi was on the line.

"You need to talk to Salinger for me. He's totally shutting me out of the investigation."

"I understand that you're frustrated," I said, "but I honestly doubt that there's anything I can do or say to sway Salinger's stance. I know he's been sharing things with me as of late, but it took a lot of effort on my part to get to this point."

"I don't see how I'm supposed to figure this whole thing out if Salinger won't tell me what he knows and Zak isn't here to help with the computer stuff."

"I know. I'm sorry things worked out the way they did."

Levi seemed really worked up, more so than I'd seen him in a long time.

"The jerk in the truck could have killed Ellie." Levi had lowered his voice.

"I know."

"She's trying to be brave, but I can tell she's in a lot of pain. I can't let that scumbag get away with this."

"I can call Salinger," I offered, "but I doubt it will do any good."

"When are you guys coming home?" Levi asked.

Good question. I'd already shown Jake everything there was to show him and he seemed more than capable of handling Sitka without my help. There really wasn't any reason for Zak and me to stay.

"There's a pretty bad storm going on at the moment, so I doubt Coop will be able to land in Moosehead," I explained. "I'll have Zak check the forecast and then call Coop and compare it with his availability. Initially, we planned to stay until the third, so I'm not sure if Coop will be able to make time to come back before then."

Levi sighed. "It would be great if you could ask."

"I will. And I should probably check with the local law enforcement to verify that there isn't a problem with us leaving earlier than planned. If Orson says it's okay and the storm lets up and Coop is available, I don't see why we can't come home sooner rather than later."

"Thanks," Levi said. "That would be very helpful."

After I hung up I got up and walked over to the desk where Zak was working. "How's it going?" I asked as I nuzzled his neck.

"Slowly." Zak groaned as I made my way around to his lips.

"Maybe you should take a break," I suggested.

Zak stood up and picked me up. He carried me over to the bed and lay me on top of it. "I think a break is exactly what I need."

Chapter 7

Monday, December 29

I lay awake, unable to sleep in spite of the fact that I should be exhausted. As I tried to count invisible sheep, a really terrible plan formed in my mind.

I'd spoken to Mary earlier and she'd indicated that Orson Kingman had left shortly after Zak and I had the previous morning and hadn't been back. He hadn't said anything to her about returning to the inn or about interviewing Zak and me or anyone else he had yet to speak to. That told me it probably wouldn't be a problem for Zak and me to leave early if the storm let up. It also indicated that he hadn't taken the time to search Colin Michaels's room. At least not thoroughly. I knew the body had been removed, but if you asked me, local law enforcement was a lot more interested in bundt cake than murder investigation.

Zak was snoring softly next to me and Charlie was curled up at the foot of the bed. Charlie looked up briefly when I slid quietly out of bed, but I put a finger to my lips and he lowered his head and went back to sleep. I pulled on a robe and slipped my feet into a pair of slippers; then, as quietly as a mouse, I slipped out of the room.

The inn was quiet as the residents slept. I knew the outer doors had been locked up tight, as they had been every night since we'd been there. No one had checked out since we'd arrived, which meant, I realized, we were most likely locked in with a killer.

The room Zak and I shared was on the top floor, the fourth story of the building and the third level of bedrooms. My destination, Colin's room, was on the second story of the inn, the first level of bedrooms. There was no elevator in the building, so I'd need to tiptoe silently down the hall and then down two flights of stairs.

Luckily for me, the room was unlocked. I slipped in as quietly as was humanly possible and then clicked on the light on my phone. I kept the light focused toward the ground so it wouldn't be seen from outside the window. Not that there was anyone outside to see the light; the storm had returned with a vengeance and it was the middle of the night, so it was highly unlikely there would be anyone lurking around outdoors.

I looked around the room, which was much like the one I shared with Zak. There was a large bed, a long dresser, a private bath, a small sitting area, and unlit fireplace. Without the warmth provided by a fire, the room was chilly, but I didn't plan to spend a lot of time there, so I figured it didn't really matter.

The man who had been staying in the room before his death had left four suitcases lined up against the far wall. A cursory glance indicated that he'd unpacked the bags and moved his clothes into the closet and dresser drawers. The bathroom cabinet contained his toiletries, which didn't seem to provide any clues. There was a small stack of books on the bedside table, mostly mysteries.

The closet contained several pairs of dress pants, as well as a few dress shirts. I doubted he'd need those in Moosehead, but perhaps this little town was just one stop on a longer journey. There were two ties and a belt on a hanger and three pairs of shoes had been placed on the floor, including a pair of snow boots.

The dresser contained more casual clothes, as well as undergarments and pj's. So far I hadn't found a single possession that might indicate a reason the man had been murdered. On top of the dresser was an expensive camera with a zoom lens. I was certain Colin Michaels would be able to take some pretty spectacular shots of the wildlife in the area with a lens the size of the one he had brought on his trip.

There was a laptop sitting on the desk near the window that I figured I might as well borrow; otherwise, the room revealed very little about the man who had stayed in it. I was about to return to my room when a little voice prompted me to look inside the suitcases, which I'd assumed had been emptied when Colin put his stuff away.

The first three cases were indeed empty, but the fourth case held something I wasn't expecting to find: a smaller case that, unfortunately, was locked. I looked around the room for a logical hiding place to keep the key. It wasn't in the suitcase where the case had been. I looked through the pockets of the other suitcases as well, but my search turned up empty. I went through all the dresser drawers and looked through the medicine cabinet in the bathroom. Logic told me the key must be somewhere in the room, unless Colin had it on him when he died. The more I thought about it, the more I realized that the key to the case was most likely at the morgue with his other personal possessions.

I decided to take the case as well as the computer back to the room I shared with Zak. There must be something I could use to pry open the container, and I was sure the computer would be the key to finding the killer.

"Zak, wake up." I nudged my sleeping fiancé as soon as I made my way back to our room.

"What's wrong?" Zak sat up abruptly.

"Nothing's wrong."

"Then why did you wake me up?"

"I need help with this case."

"Case?"

I explained my late-night snoop fest and the resulting treasure.

"I'm not sure you should have been breaking into the murder victim's room," Zak warned me.

"I didn't break in. The door was open. Now, will you help me open this or not?"

"Yeah." Zak sighed.

He got out of bed and tossed another log on the fire. Then he pulled on his own robe and slippers and began sorting through our luggage for something to use to pry open the small case. After a few minutes he came back to the bed and sat down on the edge. He began to work the lock with his pocket knife. It took a few moments, but eventually the lock gave way. Zak opened the case.

"Oh, my," I gasped.

Inside the case were dozens of photographs. Many were of the people staying at the inn, while others had been taken at different locations.

Zak frowned. "It looks like Colin has been spying on some of the other guests who are staying here."

"Why?" I wondered.

"I wish I knew. Chances are if we could figure that out we could figure out who killed him."

Zak turned on the computer and attempted to log on, but the device was password protected. I sat cross-legged on the bed and sorted through the photos while Zak unsuccessfully tried a few tricks. There were photos of every guest currently staying at the inn. If I had to guess, the photos had been taken within the week before Colin had been found dead. There were also photos of other people in other locations. All the photos were date-stamped within the past two months.

"This guy knew what he was doing, so hacking in isn't going to be easy," Zak decided. "It's too late and I'm too tired. Maybe I can work on it tomorrow."

"Yeah, okay." There was little I could do at two a.m., so I set the box on the bedside table and then cuddled up with Zak to get a few hours' sleep.

When we went down for breakfast the next morning everyone except the newlyweds, Barry and Stella Ward, were gathered around the large dining table enjoying the buffet Mary had set out. Initially, I was surprised to see everyone in attendance, but upon reflection, I realized that with the storm raging outside, no one was going skiing or anywhere else.

Marty and Mary sat at the end of the table closest to the kitchen. Next to Mary sat an older woman I had yet to meet but realized by the process of elimination must be Ethel Montros, the wealthy heiress who lived in the room next to the one where Zak and I were staying when she wasn't traveling. She was a tall and elegant woman who seemed to command attention by her very presence. I was willing to bet she'd been quite the beauty when she was younger.

Bart Lansing, the retired history professor who was at the inn to write his memoirs and who I'd met the morning after finding Colin Michaels's body, sat on Ethel's other side. He seemed to be focused intently on his meal, not paying the least bit of attention to the conversations going on around him.

Grover Wood, the geologist, sat next to Marty. The two were quite involved in a conversation having to do with hockey. There was a distinguished-looking gentleman I realized must be mystery writer Drake Rutherford sitting next to him. To Drake's left were two empty chairs. There were also two empty chairs on Bart Lansing's right.

At the other end of the table sat Jerid Richardson, Turner Hawthorn, and Liza Aldren. It made sense that they had become friends; they'd been skiing together all week. It also made sense that the longer-term residents would have established something of a bond.

"Help yourself to the buffet and then go ahead and sit anywhere," Mary instructed.

I filled my plate with eggs, toast, and fruit and then sat down next to Liza, which put Zak next to Drake. The other choice would have been to sit next to either Bart or Jerid, but I'd already spoken to Bart and was fairly certain he wasn't the killer, and I didn't like the way Jerid was leering at me. I could have sat next to Drake, but that would have put Zak next to Liza, and there was no way I was going to do that.

The first thing I noticed when I sat down beside Liza was that she had a plate full of food. Whoever said that models never ate had obviously never met the six-foot-tall supermodel.

"So how was the skiing yesterday?" I asked the group at my end of the table.

"Not bad, considering that we had the wind to deal with," Jerid replied.

"Actually, it sucked," Liza corrected him. "Jerid is just happy because the hot helicopter pilot asked him to a party."

"Jealous?" Jerid teased.

"Not even a tiny little bit."

I found it interesting that the pair seemed to have such a relaxed relationship with each other if they'd just met this week. It struck me as much more likely the pair had known each other before arriving at the inn.

"And how was your day?" I asked Turner.

"It wasn't great, but it also wasn't the worst conditions I've skied in."

So much for casual conversation. I turned toward Zak, who was deep into a discussion about the effects of climate change with the group at his end of the table.

"So are you all going to the New Year's Party at the tavern?" I tried again.

My question was met with varying degrees of uncertainty among the group.

"I wonder if Barry and Stella realize breakfast is being served," I said.

Jerid snickered. "Doubt we'll see them today after the way they were going at it all last night."

I found this interesting not because newlyweds wouldn't go at it all night but because Jerid was staying in room 2A, while the newlyweds were in 2C.

There was a room between them, so I doubted he'd heard anything from his room. Zak and I, on the other hand, were in 3C, right on top of them, and I hadn't heard a thing. I wasn't sure if this observation was important, but it seemed worth noting.

"Do you ski?" Liza asked me after shooting a look of disapproval at Jerid.

"I do," I informed her. It seemed apparent that she was trying to shut Jerid up, though I wasn't sure if it was because she was as put off by his demeanor as I was or if she was afraid he was going to say something she didn't want him to.

"You should come up with us if this storm lets up. I'm sure Jerid would be willing to sit out to make room for you."

"Hell no," Jerid said. "Turner can sit out. He spends half the time on his backside anyway."

"Stuff it," Turner responded.

"Have you been here before?" I asked Liza.

"A couple of times to Alaska, but this is my first time in Moosehead. The skiing is pretty awesome and the guy who owns the tavern is a babe, so I imagine I'll be back."

"It's such a shame what happened to Colin," I tried.

"I don't know." Liza shrugged. "The guy kept looking at me. Gave me the creeps. Personally, I'm glad I'm not stuck here with him during the storm."

"The guy was a bit of an oddball," Turner agreed.

"I would think the way you dress that you're used to men staring at you," Jerid commented.

"Bite me," Liza snapped back.

After breakfast Zak and I returned to our room while most of the others broke up into groups to watch a movie or play cards.

"So did you learn anything?" I asked.

"I think I've narrowed things down a bit," Zak answered.

"Okay, tell me what you learned and then I'll share my observations with you," I suggested.

"Ethel Montros is an interesting woman who has traveled the world and has met many of the same people I have in my travels. In fact, we decided we were most likely at the same party in Paris three years ago. While she might or might not have had a motive to murder Colin and she's certainly tall enough to have done it, I doubt she'd have the strength to pull it off. I'd take her off the suspect list, along with Mary and Bart, who are both too short."

"And Marty?" I asked.

"He's definitely tall and strong enough. I can't see that he had a motive, but the murder did happen in his inn and the victim did have photos of all of his guests. My gut says he isn't our guy, but I wouldn't remove him from the suspect list at this point. As for the others, Drake Rutherford and Grover Wood both have the physical attributes to have strangled Colin."

"What about motives?" I asked.

"I'm not sure, but I have an odd feeling about both men. Wood claims to be a visiting geologist, but when I mentioned Landon Stanford's name he showed no indication of ever having heard it before."

"And Landon is a geologist," I realized. "He has to be our killer."

"Maybe, maybe not. What's certain is that he probably isn't really a geologist."

"What about Drake?" I asked. "The guy is famous. I doubt he's a killer."

"Why not?" Zak asked. "He kills people for a living."

"In his books," I pointed out.

"True, but when I brought up Colin's death he acted odd."

"Odd how?" I asked.

Zak shook his head as he appeared to be trying to put his finger on it. "I'm not sure I can describe it. Let's just say I got an odd vibe. I wouldn't take him off the list just yet."

"Okay, so we have Marty, Grover, and Drake," I summarized.

"How about your group?" Zak asked.

"Jerid is an ass. I'm not saying that makes him a killer, but he's an ass, and he has a strange thing going on with Liza. I'm pretty sure they knew each other before they came to Moosehead for the holiday. There's just too much animosity between them to have just met."

"You think they're in on it together?" Zak asked.

"Not necessarily. They don't seem like they have the kind of relationship that would cause them to want to work together. My money is on Jerid acting alone. Like I said, he's an ass."

"Okay, for argument's sake let's say it isn't Jerid. Would you lean toward Turner or Liza?"

I frowned. "I don't know. Turner's a hard read. He never said much of anything. Physically, he could have done it, but I couldn't get enough out of him to hint at a motive. As for Liza, she's certainly tall enough, and she said Colin kept staring at her. Still, she must be used to pervs checking her out, so I can't see that as a motive for murder. She did seem glad the guy was dead, though, so it's possible she could have some other motive. Still, I don't know what that might be."

"Actually, she has the best motive of all, along with Drake," Zak asserted.

I sat back and scrunched up my face. "How so?"

"Both Liza and Drake have very public reputations to uphold. Reputations that could greatly affect very high-profile careers that bring them millions of dollars a year. Colin had photos of everyone at the inn. Lots of photos."

"So maybe he had photos of either Liza or Drake doing something they didn't want getting out. Maybe he was blackmailing one of them." I finally caught on.

"Exactly."

I looked out the window. The snow was still coming down in white sheets. It was beautiful but confining. All Zak and I had managed to do was eliminate Ethel, Mary, and Bart as possible suspects. The murder could have been committed by any of the others, including the newlyweds. They'd told everyone they were there on their honeymoon, but that could just be a cover. For all we knew, they were hired guns or serial killers. And it was a little odd that they hadn't come down for breakfast. Even newlyweds needed to eat, and with the weather, it was doubtful they planned to go into town for a bite.

"I wish the snow would let up," I commented. "I really wanted to show the photos we found in Colin's room to Jake and Harmony. It would be interesting to get their take on this whole thing. I'm not sure how all of this is related, but it would just be too strange if

Colin's murder, Gary's death, and Devon's disappearance five years ago aren't related. One thing is for sure: I'm going to go out on a limb and say that Colin isn't a traveling salesman who happens to be passing through town like he told Marty and Mary."

"I guess we could call Jake," Zak suggested.

"That's a good idea. Maybe he'll have some input."

"Why don't you call over to the tavern and I'll hop on the computer to see if I can find out who Colin Michaels really is?"

"What if Colin Michaels isn't his real name?" I asked.

"It'll be harder to track him down but not impossible. I noticed that several of his photos were taken in Tokyo, and another one in Moscow. There were also photos taken in Washington DC. Maybe we can figure out where he'd been before he showed up at in Moosehead."

"How do you know where the photos were taken?" I asked.

"I've been all those places and recognized the scenery in the background. The photos are date-stamped. I'm betting we can map his route fairly accurately. That might not tell us who he is, but it will show where he's been."

Chapter 8

I called Jake who, as I suspected, was very interested in the photos. He suggested that he come pick Zak and me up and take us back to the tavern, which was closed for the day, so we could speak without the danger of being overheard. We arranged for him to get us in an hour's time.

After I hung up with Jake I called Salinger, as I'd promised Levi I would. I doubted it would do any good, but at least I could honestly say I'd tried.

"If it isn't Zoe Donovan," Sheriff Salinger greeted me. "You back in Ashton Falls?"

"No, I'm still in Alaska. Big blizzard; double homicide."

"Ah. I should have known. You do seem to attract the corpses."

"Very funny."

"Does the local law enforcement know you like to snoop around?" Salinger asked.

"The subject hasn't come up, but between you and me, he'd be lucky to have my help."

"Oh, and why is that?"

"I don't think the guy is all that sharp of a cop. The man showed up at the crime scene in his pajamas."

Salinger chuckled. "You yankin' my chain?"

"Nope. Blue and gray plaid flannel."

Salinger laughed out loud. "Sounds like my kind of town. Now, what can I do for you?"

"The reason I'm calling is because I'm concerned about Levi. He's really frustrated about not being able to track down the man who ran him off the road and is a little cranky because you won't work with him. I realize you and Levi don't have the relationship you and I do, but I was hoping maybe you could throw him a bone."

My request was met with silence on the other end of the line.

"Salinger, are you there?" I asked.

"I'm here."

"So? Can you help me out here? Ellie said he's climbing the walls trying to solve this case."

I could hear the man breathing, but he wasn't speaking. I decided to wait until he thought through my request.

"I'm going to tell you something I don't think you should tell your friend," Salinger finally said. "The only reason I'm telling you this is because you'll probably have your boyfriend hack into my files if I don't give you something to gnaw on."

"He would never." My denial sounded lame even to me.

"Yeah, right. Here's the thing: We've identified the man who set the fire at the lumberyard and ran your friends off the road. His name is Poke Blane and he's a guard at the prison where Buck Stevenson was incarcerated. Or at least he *was* a guard at the prison. Something happened that I have yet to figure out that caused him to quit two weeks ago after twenty years on the job. Mr. Stevenson swears he has no idea why the man did what he did, but I haven't quite made up my mind whether I believe him. What I do know is that your friend is a hothead who would probably throw himself in front of a moving vehicle if he thought it would get him the answers he wants. I think we both know that if he learns the identity of the man who almost killed him and the little lady who was with him, he'll go after the guy and probably end up good and dead."

I realized Salinger wasn't wrong. Levi was being irrational when it came to the accident. "So what do I do?" I asked. "Levi isn't just going to give up. He'll keep looking until he figures out who the guy is."

"If he were my friend I'd give him a decoy."

"Decoy?" I asked.

"Lie to him. Tell him you spoke to me and I gave you a clue. Tell him something that will send him on a wild-goose chase in the wrong direction until we can find the man we're after and lock him safely away."

I hated to admit it, but Salinger's idea wasn't all that bad.

"Do you think the man is still in the area?" I asked.

"It's hard to say. My guess is that he would have left after setting the fire, but it makes no sense that he would run your friends off the road. All that did was bring attention to himself and provide us with a really good clue as to the identity of our arsonist."

"So you have no idea where to find him?" I asked.

"I did have one lead, but it turned out to be a bust. One of the clerks at the Ashton Falls Motor Inn claimed to have seen a man in a black truck hanging around the past few days. I checked into it, but it turned out to be a dead end. When we tracked him down we found out he was simply a married man meeting a lady friend at the facility. I'm pretty sure our arsonist is lying low. He's either staying out of the area or he's rented a house with a garage so his vehicle won't be visible."

"Yeah, but the fact that he ran Levi and Ellie off the road makes it seem like he wants to get caught."

"Yeah, maybe. All I know for certain is that the man isn't acting rationally, which in my opinion makes him more dangerous."

"Okay. I'll try to send Levi in the wrong direction. And Salinger, if Levi gets too close, lock him up. I'd rather he be behind bars than dead."

"Ten four, and you take care of yourself as well. Can I help?"

I laughed. Talk about a strange turn of events. Salinger was offering to help *me* with *my* investigation? "Maybe," I answered. "Zak is working on a few things, but if he comes up empty I might call you back. For now, just track down this Poke Blane and lock him up before Levi finds him."

After hanging up with Salinger I decided to call Ellie and Levi. Part of me wanted to tell Ellie what was going on so I could enlist her help in misdirecting Levi, but the other part realized that asking her to lie to her boyfriend really wasn't a fair thing to do. I figured I'd talk to Ellie first to get a feel for the situation and then decide what to say to Levi.

"Zoe, I'm so glad you called," Ellie said as soon as she answered her cell.

"Why? What's up?" I recognized the sound of panic in her voice.

"It's Levi. He got a lead about a black truck at the Ashton Falls Motor Inn and took off before I could stop him."

I realized the cheating husband was as good a diversion as any. "You know, I just talked to Salinger, and he mentioned he'd had a report of a black truck there as well."

"What if Levi runs into the guy? It isn't going to be pretty, broken arm or not."

"There are a lot of black trucks in the area," I tried to reassure Ellie. "The chances of the black truck at the inn being the same one that ran you off the road are slim."

"Yeah, I guess. I wish you and Zak were here. I'm having a hard time keeping Levi from going all Rambo."

"The good news is that Salinger has a lead he hopes will pan out. If it does things should be wrapped up in no time."

"Lead? What lead?"

"He wouldn't say." I crossed my fingers, like I did when I was a child and told a white lie. "He sounded like he had everything under control, though. You know, I think with all the murders we've had lately he's really had a chance to practice his investigation techniques. I think he's coming along."

Ellie laughed. "Do you know how ridiculous you sound?"

"Yeah." I giggled. "I guess I do sound silly. How's your leg?"

"It itches. I have to tell you, I'm way over the whole cast thing. I want to take a nice long bath. I *need* to take a nice long bath," Ellie emphasized.

"What did Dr. Westlake say about baths?"

"Don't."

"You aren't supposed to bathe at all until the cast comes off?"

"He gave me a plastic thing to put over the cast if I want to shower, but I'm not sure I can manage it on my own. I really need to wash my hair."

"So have Levi help you out. I bet that will distract him from the investigation for a while."

I could almost picture Ellie grinning.

"Yeah, I guess it would distract him at that. By the way, have you heard about the hullabaloo at the high school?"

"No, what's going on at the high school?"

"It seems there was an emergency meeting called this morning. The faculty is trying to figure out how to deal with the staff shortage created by the whole mess over Christmas."

"They must have at least three positions to fill. School starts back up on the fifth, right? What are they planning to do?"

"There's a plan to use a substitute teacher to fill in for Mrs. Jolly until a permanent replacement can be found. I guess Boomer's position was seen as a luxury, so they're just going to leave it unfilled for the time being. The real problem is that now that Lamé is good and fired, they have to deal with the prospect of replacing the principal in just a few days."

Mrs. Jolly, a teacher, had been murdered before Christmas, and during the investigation into her death, improper conduct on the part of Principal Lamé had come to light. Boomer, who had been Levi's assistant coach, was fired after it came out that he was providing steroids to some of the athletes.

"So what are they going to do?" I asked.

"They've assigned two teachers to take over the admin duties. One of them is Levi."

"Really?" I had to admit I was surprised. Levi had spent a lot of time in the principal's office, both as a student and as a staff member after becoming a coach and physical education teacher, but all of that time had been spent on the wrong side of the desk.

"Yeah. Levi was shocked when they asked him to do it, but they pointed out that now that football season was over he had a lighter load than most."

"Yeah, but when baseball starts up . . ."

"It could be a problem," Ellie acknowledged. "At first Levi was pretty unhappy with the idea, but then I reminded him that he's been complaining about some of the policies at the school for years, so this could be his chance to make some changes. After he thought about it he realized this was a good opportunity."

"Who's the other teacher who's going to take over the administration duties along with him?" I asked.

"A new English teacher I haven't met yet. Her name is Jillian Frank."

Uh-oh. I knew Jillian. She was young, beautiful, and single, and I'd seen her noticing Levi on more than one occasion. Ellie wasn't going to be happy when she found out.

"Levi is going to go over to her house one day this week to come up with a plan for exactly how to carry out the new duties they've been assigned," Ellie added. "He seemed bummed to be asked to miss out on even more of his winter vacation than he already has, but I'm glad he has something else to fret over other than the idiot who ran us off the road."

"And how long is this temporary assignment supposed to last?" I wondered.

"Levi thinks it could be the rest of the school year. I guess the process of hiring a new principal is a lengthy procedure that could take months."

"Yeah, I imagine they have to officially post the position, do interviews, and conduct background searches. Still, maybe they'll get lucky and find someone sooner rather than later."

"Maybe," Ellie said. "By the way, did you hear that Kelly's sister is getting married?"

Kelly was Ellie's assistant at the Beach Hut. I hadn't heard, so we chatted about the wedding and other inconsequential things for the next twenty minutes, with me making an effort to divert her attention from Levi and his new job, as well as his ill-conceived errand. I hoped the dynamic created by Levi and Jillian working so closely together wouldn't become an issue for the new couple. I'd decided not to bring up the fact that Jillian was single and gorgeous at that point; Ellie had enough to worry about with Levi and his determination to track down a killer.

"It sounds like Levi is back. Will you talk to him?" Ellie asked.

"Yeah, put him on."

I tried to formulate a plan that would send my best friend in the wrong direction. I loved Levi, but I didn't want him getting arrested or worse. Salinger was correct in his assertion that Levi could be a bit of a hothead at times.

"Hey, Zoe. What's up?" Levi was out of breath, as if he'd been running prior to answering the phone.

I filled him in on the murder investigation in Moosehead and then asked him about his own investigation in Ashton Falls.

"It's been frustrating," Levi admitted. "Salinger refuses to work with me and I'm having a hard time coming up with leads without Zak's help. I had a lead on a black truck at the motor inn, but it turned out to be a bust."

"I spoke to Salinger," I offered. "He said he had reason to believe that the man who ran you off the road might have left the area."

"How could he possibly know that?" Levi countered.

"I guess he can't know for certain, but there's been no sign of him since it happened, so I guess it makes sense that the guy could have fled."

"Yeah, maybe. But on the off chance that he's still around, I'm going to keep looking. Let's face it: I really don't have anything better to do than drive around and look for him."

"What about Ellie?" I asked.

"What about her?"

"Maybe she would appreciate you sticking around for company."

Levi was silent.

"I'm sure it's been hard on her, not being able to get around," I added.

"Yeah. I guess."

"If you promise to stay put I'll see if I can get Zak to do a DMV search. Did you happen to notice the make of the truck or anything specific about the license plate? Was it local?"

I got everything from Levi that he could remember and promised to have Zak do the computer search, and Levi promised to hang tight until I could get back to him. Salinger and I already knew who the truck belonged to, so a DMV search would be pointless, but Levi didn't, and I needed to buy some time for the sheriff to catch up with the guy.

Chapter 9

Jake picked us up and we found Harmony and Dani waiting for us when we arrived at the tavern. Jordan was working at the clinic, but she had called Jake earlier that morning to tell him that Gary Peterman hadn't been murdered. According to the autopsy results, the man had suffered a major heart attack and died almost instantly. That didn't tell us why Gary was in Moosehead in the first place, or why he was wandering around in a storm. It also didn't explain how he happened to have a recent photo of a man everyone believed had died five years before. But mostly it didn't help us to figure out why Devon left in the first place, or where he'd been all that time.

Dani was understandably upset by the whole thing, but the truth of the matter was that, short of discovering a new clue, there was no way to answer those questions, so the group decided to work on the mystery they might be able to solve: who killed Colin Michaels?

"Here's what I know," Zak began after Jake had finished filling us in and turned the floor over to him. "Colin Michaels probably isn't a traveling salesman. Assuming he personally took all the photos we found in the case—which, in all fairness, we don't know for certain—the man has been to London, Rome, Paris, Moscow, Tokyo, and Washington DC, in the past several months."

"The guy gets around," Harmony commented as Whiskey climbed into her lap.

"Yeah, and those are all major cities," Dani pointed out. "What's a guy like that doing in Moosehead?"

"I have a few theories, none of which I can prove quite yet," Zak answered.

"He must be a spy," Harmony offered.

"Or a terrorist," I provided.

"He could be some sort of smuggler," Dani postulated.

"Or a reporter," Jake said.

"A reporter?" I asked. "Seems like a stretch."

"No, the man was a reporter," Jake clarified. He turned his computer around so that the others at the table could see the screen. "His name was Carter Christianson. He was a freelance investigative reporter who uncovered some pretty big scandals in his day. When you showed me his photo I thought he looked familiar, but I wasn't certain."

"I've heard of him." Zak nodded. "He'd written some pretty important stuff, and he wasn't afraid to get his hands dirty to get the dirt he needed."

"Get his hands dirty to get the dirt." I laughed.

Harmony was the only one to join in. At least someone had a sense of humor.

"Okay, so if the man who died in the inn is really Carter Christianson, why was he here in Moosehead?" Dani asked. "It doesn't seem to fit his usual profile at all."

"Good question," Zak acknowledged.

"Carter was known for digging into the bowels of society to find the stories no one wanted told. He must have been closing in on someone and followed that person to Moosehead," Jake offered.

"Someone staying at the Inn," Zak added.

"But he must not have known exactly who it was he was after, only that they'd be staying at the inn," I realized. Charlie looked up when I spoke with such a high level of excitement in my voice. It was good to be able to add to the conversation.

"Why do you say that?" Harmony asked.

"Because he was taking photos of everyone at the inn. He must have been trying to figure out which guest was the guy or girl he was after."

"Zoe has a point," Zak supported. "There are photos of everyone. My guess is that he got intel that the person he was looking for would be staying at the inn, but he didn't know what the person looked like, and we can assume the target was registered under an alias."

"This is just too strange." Dani shook her head. "First a high-profile reporter is murdered in our little town and then I find out that after all these years Devon is alive. My logical mind tells me the two incidents must be linked in some way, but Devon was just a regular guy who came to Moosehead to work at the hunting lodge at the base of the mountain for the summer. We met and fell in love and he decided to stay. How can this sweet, regular guy be tied into whatever it is that got this investigative reporter killed?"

Jake reached out and covered Dani's hand with his own. "If Gary's presence in Moosehead with a photo of Devon and Carter Christianson's murder are related in some way, chances are that your fiancé was never really a regular guy."

Dani looked down at the table. This had to be so hard on her—to be in love with someone and then find out he never was who you thought he was. I really couldn't imagine. Zak grabbed my hand under the table and gave it a squeeze. I looked at him and frowned. Could my super-rich, world-traveling, always-away-at-business-meetings fiancé be a spy or a member of a drug cartel or a diamond smuggler? Nah. Not Zak. He was such a regular guy. I looked at Dani, realizing she'd believed the exact same thing about the man she loved.

"Maybe Devon really was exactly who he seemed to be," I offered. "Maybe he came to Moosehead to work at the lodge and ended up falling in love. Everyone has said that Gary was an odd sort. What if Gary was the one who wasn't who he said he was and Devon just got caught in the crossfire?"

Dani frowned. She looked up at me. "You think?"

"It's possible."

Jake sat back in his chair. "I don't think we can figure out what happened to Devon or why he left without more information. A lot more. But I do think we can figure out who killed Carter. Zak has stated that it had to be one of the fourteen people who were staying at the inn on the night the murder was committed. That's a pretty small pool."

Jake looked at Dani. "I know this is hard for you, and I understand that you want to figure out what happened to Devon, but our best bet at finding any answers is to solve the mystery that seems to be the most likely to be solved."

"Jake is right," Zak declared. "It shouldn't be that hard to narrow down the suspect field. Dani has been skiing with most of them, and Zoe and I have talked to everyone who's in residence. We have names and photos of everyone. Let's see what we can find out."

Dani looked at the group. "Okay. Do you have another computer I can use?"

"I do." Jake got up to fetch it.

Harmony and I decided to make everyone lunch while the whiz kids worked on finding out what they could about the people on our list. Charlie and Whiskey followed us into the warm and inviting kitchen while Sitka chose to stay behind with Jake. It seemed Whiskey had stopped growling at Charlie; the two were almost acting like buddies.

"They're pretty intense in there," I observed. Zak, Jake, and Dani all had their heads down and were typing frantically.

"Yeah. They're all really smart. Landon too. Usually it's Wyatt who's my kitchen buddy."

"Where are Landon and Wyatt today?" I asked.

"Landon is working and Wyatt didn't answer his cell when Jake called. I'm pretty sure he has a new woman of the week."

"Woman of the week?"

"Yeah. Wyatt is a great guy, but he likes variety, so he usually only hooks up with women who are here on vacation and leaving within the week."

"I have a friend who used to be a lot like that, but he's in a relationship now that I think could go the distance. Should I start slicing that bread?" I asked.

"Yeah, that would be helpful."

"Do you think Dani's going to be okay?" I asked. "It must be so weird to find out that the man you loved and believed dead is really alive. I think if that happened to me it would destroy the very foundation of my life."

Harmony stopped what she was doing. "Honestly, I'm worried about her. Dani is a beautiful woman who knows how to show off her assets. She has guys panting after her all the time. When you look at her, you probably think she has a new guy every night, but the reality is just the opposite. Dani is a private person who keeps her emotions close. Devon was the only guy she dated seriously, and I know she really loved him. When the team couldn't find him, she completely fell apart. It took her a long time to get on with her life. I can't imagine what she's going through now."

I looked through the open door to the other room. Dani appeared to be completely focused on the computer in front of her, but I didn't see how she could be. Everything she believed in had turned out to be a lie. How can anyone ever recover from that?

"Do you think she'll look for him?" I asked.

Harmony frowned. "I don't know. He knows where she is, where she's been for the past five years. If he wanted to get in touch with her, he could have. He has to have known what it would do to her to believe he was dead and he left anyway. If it were me, I'm not sure I'd bother to look for him. But Dani? I don't know. Maybe."

I set aside the bread and began slicing cheese. "You guys are lucky to have one another. You seem like more than just a team. You're more like a family who really cares about one another."

"We are." Harmony smiled. "Jake, Dani, Wyatt, and I are pretty much alone in the world. Jordan has a sister who lives in town. She's married with kids and is really great, but their parents passed a while back, so it's just them. Landon's family moved to Vermont a long time ago. They aren't really close. The six of us aren't *like* a family, we *are* a family."

Before Harmony and I could even get the food on the table the phone rang, and the entire team jumped into action. A six-year-old had wandered away from the rental home his family was staying in for the week and hadn't been seen in over an hour. Harmony flipped a switch, which sent a siren blaring loud enough for people to hear it for miles around. Dani gathered warm outerwear for everyone while Jake and Jordan rolled out a map and discussed a strategy. Landon, Wyatt, and at least twenty other people showed up before I could even put the food away. Jake consulted with Landon and then divided everyone up into teams. Each team was assigned a grid based on the location of the last sighting of the boy. Before I could comment about the efficiency with which the rescue team was deployed, everyone except for Harmony was out the door and headed into the storm.

Zak went with Jake and the crew, while I stayed behind to help Harmony with the stragglers who were still arriving to help out. Tension was high as everyone battled with their own thoughts of what could come to pass if the child wasn't found soon.

"Is it always like this?" I asked.

"Every time is different, but, yeah, when a child's life is at stake everyone pitches in."

"How do the townsfolk know what type of emergency is going on?" I asked as Harmony set up the radio.

"The siren is different for different events. Blue team, do you copy?" Harmony said into the microphone.

"Copy." I recognized Wyatt's voice. "Visibility is zero, so we're executing a shoulder-to-shoulder line."

"Copy that. Red team?"

I felt helpless as I watched Harmony check in with each team leader. Due to the severity of the storm, rescue workers were lined up with only a small space between each person. The last thing they needed was for the rescuers to need rescuing. I noticed that Sitka had left with Jake, and I was happy to see that he seemed to know exactly what to do.

As members of the community wandered in, I served coffee and sandwiches and did what I could to make the frantic parents, who had arrived shortly after the team left, as comfortable as possible. I quickly saw that Harmony was good at what she did. When she'd first told me that she stayed behind to man the radios I thought the team had given her a lesser job because of her age, but after watching her perform under fire I could see she was the driver who steered the bus. She knew where everyone was and where they should be. She both took and gave direction as was required. By the end of the night I had a newfound respect for my new friend in the north.

"Yellow team, come in."

"Go for yellow," Dani replied.

"Red team is going to continue down to the lake, so take your team and head toward the gully. Green team will come from the other direction and meet up with you at Dingman's fence."

"Ten four."

"Green, did you copy?" Harmony asked.

"Copy," Landon replied.

Harmony made a few notes and picked the mic back up. "Base to Purple."

"Go for Purple," Jordan replied.

"Status report."

"Temps are dropping and the snow isn't letting up. Based on TOE, I'd say thirty to forty-five."

"Ten four."

"TOE?" I asked.

"Time of exposure," Harmony informed me. "Basically, it's the time we estimate the rescue victim has been exposed to the elements."

"I thought he'd been missing an hour when the parents called in."

"He had," Harmony confirmed.

"But Jordan said thirty to forty-five?"

"That's the amount of time in minutes he most likely has left before critical hypothermia sets in."

Oh God.

"Red team, what is your forty?"

"Far side of Anderson's field. So far it isn't looking good," Jake reported. "Wait. Sitka has something."

I held my breath as I waited for Jake to come back on the line. Each second seemed like an eternity as I waited to find out the fate of the child. Both of the child's parents were crying as members of the community who weren't out in the storm prayed with them that their son would be returned to them alive and well.

"Red team to base," Jake's voice came over the radio. "We've got him. He's alive and sporting a seventy. Purple leader, get your butt over to Anderson's field ASAP."

"On my way," Jordan replied.

Everyone in the bar broke into cheers. Most of them were crying, while a few helped themselves to Jake's bar stock for a toast.

"What's a seventy?" I asked Harmony as tears of relief streamed down my own face.

"It's a code for condition. A seventy is good, considering. A person can be alive and near death. They'd be a ten. Someone who's completely unharmed would be a ninety. It's a way to let the team know what to expect without breaking bad news to the family, who may be listening in over the radio."

Harmony stood up to stretch and I hugged her with all my might. "You, my friend, are really something."

Harmony looked shocked at the compliment. "Thanks, but I didn't do anything."

"Harmony, my girl, you did *everything*."

Chapter 10

Tuesday, December 30

The next morning I sat at the counter in the kitchen at the inn, watching as Mary made pumpkin spice pull-apart bread, which, she informed me, was a recipe she had gotten from her good friend Jade. Zak had gone with Marty to exercise the sled dogs and Charlie had wanted to go with him. I was sure Zak would end up carrying Charlie for most of the hike, but I was equally certain Zak wouldn't mind in the least.

The storm that had raged the day before had slowed to a gentle flurry this morning, so Dani had come by earlier to pick up the skiers staying on the third floor. Ethel had stayed in her room, requesting that a breakfast tray be brought to her. Mary explained that at times Ethel's arthritis caught up with her and she had to take it easy.

Both Drake and Bart had retired to their rooms to write after the morning meal and I hadn't seen any sign of Grover, which left Mary and me alone on the first floor.

"Have you and Marty owned the inn long?" I asked conversationally.

"About eight years. Before that we lived in Los Angeles."

"LA to Moosehead; that's quite a change," I observed.

"It was a huge change, but one day we woke up, looked at each other, and decided we needed to find a place with clean air and clean water and a slower pace of life. We looked around for over a year before we heard about the inn. The previous owners wanted to move somewhere warmer and we wanted a small-town atmosphere, so we exchanged homes. It worked out well for all of us."

"Harmony mentioned the town tends to die in the winter. Is it tough to make a living with such a seasonal occupancy?"

"Sometimes. We're usually booked solid from June through mid-September. Then there's a lull until Thanksgiving, and we're booked until after New Year's. We're fortunate that heliskiing is so popular right now."

"I didn't realize how popular it was until I arrived here. How much snow do you get annually?"

"We get around three hundred inches in town, but the mountain can get anywhere from six hundred to nine hundred inches, which makes this part of Alaska popular with the backcountry crowd."

"I imagine there are a lot of visitors who come to the area for ice climbing and snowmobiling as well. Harmony mentioned that there weren't a lot of lodging opportunities in the winter."

"There aren't," Mary confirmed. "Moosehead is a small town that only recently has become known as a winter destination. Although the Richardson Highway provides road access to the area, once winter sets in driving the highway is treacherous at best. The motel in town closes for the season around September 15 and doesn't reopen until Memorial Day weekend, so although many skiers who come to the area tend to gravitate toward more easily accessible towns, the ones who do come to Moosehead usually stay here."

"Are you the only property that stays open year-round?"

"No, there are several lodges in the area that remain open over the winter, as well as some summer homes that can be rented by either short- or long-term visitors. This year we're fortunate to have several long-term guests. Both Bart and Drake have expressed their intention to stay through Presidents Day at least, and Ethel rents her room on an annual basis and comes and goes as she pleases."

"And Grover?" I asked. I seemed to remember that his reservation was open-ended as well.

"He checked out this morning, actually. He initially expressed an interest in staying through January, but he told me yesterday that his work was wrapping up sooner than expected."

I picked up a slice of apple that had been left on the fruit plate Mary had served for breakfast and nibbled on one end. The fact that Grover had left could complicate things; in my mind, he was at the top of the suspect list. If he was guilty of killing Carter, solving this case might not be possible. "And what exactly does Grover do for a living?"

Mary frowned and stopped what she was doing to look at me. "I'm not sure exactly. I think he's some sort of scientist. I thought he said something about being a geologist at one point, but he didn't seem to know much about the subject, so I suppose I could have been mistaken."

The warm kitchen was inviting and cozy, and the smell of the sweetbreads that were cooling on the racks were ever so inviting. Mary explained that she liked to bake once a week and then freeze the loaves until they were needed. She was mixing up the pumpkin bread but had already baked several apple walnut loaves, as well as a banana pecan and a blueberry crunch. As with most of the other rooms in the inn, the kitchen featured a wood-burning fireplace that helped to keep the room warm.

"What are your plans for the day?" Mary asked me as she took a fresh dishrag out of a drawer and wiped down the dark blue tile countertop.

"Since Zak is tied up with Marty, Harmony's going to stop by later to pick me up. We're going to go shopping for something for me to wear to the party at the tavern tomorrow night."

"Sounds like fun." Mary took one of the loaves of bread that had been cooling off on the rack, placed it on a cutting board, and began to slice it.

"I'm sure it will be, but part of me wishes I'd gone along with Marty and Zak. Dogsledding looks like a lot of fun."

"I suppose it is, if you don't mind the cold."

"Does Marty race his team?" I asked.

"He does. In fact, he's been working to build a team that will be competitive in the Iditarod."

I knew that the Iditarod was a grueling race that covered more than 1,150 miles between Anchorage and Nome. The race could last between nine and thirty days as sled teams of sixteen or more dogs traveled thorough harsh winter conditions. The idea of running in the Iditarod sounded adventurous, but I wasn't sure I could go that long without a hot shower.

"Does Marty feel like he has the dogs to win such a grueling race?" I wondered.

"He doesn't want to win; he just wants to finish. His goal is to get the red lantern."

"The red lantern?"

Mary wiped her hands on a dish towel and began putting away the items she had taken from the pantry. "During the days of Alaska sled-dog freighting and mail carrying, dog drivers relied on a series of roadhouses between their village destinations. Because those mushers had to deal with all kinds of weather, they filed a flight plan of sorts. When a musher got close to a roadhouse a kerosene lamp was lit and hung outside, which helped the dog driver find his destination at night. The lantern would remain lit until the dog team arrived. It's become a tradition to award the last-place finisher with a red lantern. At first it was sort of a joke, but the award now carries a level of prestige."

"So does Marty plan to join the race this year?"

"No; this is a building year. Besides, we have puppies, so we need to stay close to home."

"Puppies?"

"Would you like to see them?" Mary asked.

"I'd love to."

Mary checked on the bread in the oven and then we both bundled up with multiple layers of clothing and headed out the door toward the kennel.

The building was empty because Marty and Zak had taken the dogs for a run, but I could tell the animals were well cared for because the interior of the building was spotlessly clean and comfortably heated. Mary led me through the main kennel to a separate room that she referred to as the "maternity ward." The puppy nursery was kept at a warmer temperature than the main part of the kennel, to accommodate the newly born babies, I imagined. There were three separate cages that contained puppies, each one with a birthing box lined with warm, soft bedding. There was also plenty of room for the mom to leave the box to stretch her legs. In the first cage were five adorable pups who appeared to be six or seven weeks old.

"Where is their mom?" I asked as they all ran over toward where we were standing.

"Marty would have taken her out for a bit of exercise because he's not really running the team. Nanuk is one of our younger moms. This is her first litter. The pups will be weaned in the next couple of weeks and she'll return to the main part of the building."

"Are you going to keep all the pups?" I asked as the little fur balls bumped up on the gate to get our attention.

Mary laughed. "Heavens no. Marty keeps the pups who show the most potential and sells the others to reputable homes in the area. Would you like to play with them?"

"Absolutely."

Mary opened the cage and the little bundles of fur came romping out. Talk about adorable. Their coats were soft and fuzzy, and each puppy looked slightly different from his or her brothers and sisters.

"Aren't you just the cutest little thing?" I said as I picked up one of the bundles of fluff who had been biting at my feet.

"That's Miki. She's the runt of the litter, so I'm sure Marty won't keep her, but I do love the unique color of her coat."

While the other pups were varying shades of gray and white, Miki's coat was a gorgeous shade of copper.

"She really is cute. Do you screen the homes the pups go to?"

"Most times we personally know the people who buy our pups or, at the very least, the prospective owner is someone who has been referred by someone we know."

"You currently have three dogs with pups?" I noticed two other dogs watching us.

"This is Aurora," Mary introduced me to the mama in the next cage over. "Her pups are just two weeks old. This is her third and probably final litter. I know Marty has an eye on a couple of these pups as potential dogs for his team. Aurora is one of his favorite dogs, but he's thinking it might be time to retire her."

"Will you keep her?"

"Actually, we might. We've only been breeding and racing the dogs for about six years, and in that time we've only had to retire one other dog: a male named Suka. We thought about keeping him, but he wasn't the sort to really want to be a house dog, so Marty placed him with a neighbor who lives alone and has no other animals. Aurora, on the other hand, loves to come into the inn and visit when we don't have guests. She likes people and other animals, so I think she'll be able to make the transition."

"And the last cage?" I asked as I walked around to where a beautiful tricolored mama was dutifully tending to her babies.

"This is Willow. She's a second-time mom. Her pups were just born on Christmas Eve."

"Do you have pups every year?" I asked.

"No. We usually breed every other year, but it depends a bit on the particular age and cycle of the bitches Marty identifies as having breeding potential." Mary looked at her watch. "I should get back to my baking."

I was sorry to see the pups put back in their cage, but I understood that Mary had a lot to do with an inn full of guests. Maybe I'd try to come back to play with them again before we left.

Back in the inn, Mary washed up and began slicing a loaf of bread. "I'm going to head up to see if Ethel would like some bread," Mary announced. "Will you listen for the buzzer? The loaves that are in the oven will need to come out in a few minutes."

"Sure. No problem."

I took advantage of the fact that I was alone on the bottom story of the building to look around a bit. Carter Christianson's room had still been left as it was when he died and I was tempted to make a return visit, but I wasn't sure how long Mary would be tied up talking to Ethel. It occurred to me that it was odd that Ethel rented a room on the top floor of the inn if she suffered from health issues such as arthritis. The inn didn't have an elevator, so it made more sense for her to choose a room on the second floor— the first floor of bedrooms—and save herself the extra two flights of stairs every time she wanted to come down for a meal or enjoy the common rooms. The more I thought about it the more certain I was that there were a lot of strange things going on at the inn, things that were just normal enough so as not to arouse suspicion.

There was a pile of mail on the table near the front door that I couldn't resist going through. I realized once I started looking that this was outgoing mail, waiting, I assumed, for someone to make the trip into town to post it. Mostly the pile contained bills waiting to be paid, but about halfway down I found a rather thick envelope from Ethel addressed to someone living in Tokyo.

I supposed the fact that Ethel knew someone in Tokyo wasn't all that odd; she traveled for much of the year, and I imagined she had established relationships with people all over the world.

"Looks like the dog trainer is a snoop."

I turned around to find Jerid staring at me from the bottom of the stairs.

"I thought you went skiing with the others."

"I was going to, but then I decided to stay back and take care of some business I'd been meaning to deal with. Anything interesting?" he asked as he stared at the pile of mail still in my hand.

"Not at all," I said just as I heard the oven buzzer. I set the mail down where I'd found it. "Oops, almost forgot the bread," I said as I hurried away.

Chapter 11

Luckily, Harmony showed up shortly after I'd rescued Mary's bread from the oven, so I was able to avoid any further interaction with Jerid. As we drove back into town, where I hoped to find a dress for the New Year's Eve party at the tavern, I explained to Harmony what had occurred and expressed my opinion that Jerid could very well be our killer.

"The fact that Jerid caught you snooping and called you on it doesn't make him a killer," Harmony pointed out.

"I know, but the guy gives me the creeps," I argued.

"I'm sure he's harmless. He's just one of those athletic, good-looking guys who thinks he has a God-given right to elevated status over the rest of us. That elevated sense of self has turned him into something of a jerk."

"Maybe. But I wish I'd had the chance to finish looking through the mail. The guy seemed concerned that I was looking through it, which makes me suspect that he's trying to hide something," I insisted.

"If he had some kind of secret letter why wouldn't he just take it into town and post it himself?"

"Good point."

"We don't have a lot of shopping options in Moosehead, but there's a boutique that has a pretty good selection. My friend Erin owns it. I thought after we got your dress we could stop in at Chloe's place. Maybe we can have lunch. I want you to meet her."

"I'd like that."

"I think you'll like her," Harmony informed me. "She's really sweet and has a huge heart. The two of us volunteer at the local animal shelter."

"I didn't realize Moosehead had a shelter."

"We didn't used to. Chloe and I and a few other women in town decided we really needed a facility where unwanted animals could be safely cared for until new homes could be found for them. Prior to the opening of the center, abandoned animals were often dumped on the side of the road, left to fend for themselves. I managed to convince a friend of mine who had a large, unused building on a piece of property he owned to let us convert it into a shelter. We had a series of fund-raisers to purchase the material we needed to complete the conversion and the citizens of Moosehead all joined in to provide the labor. The local vet donates his services and the feed store sells us the supplies we need at cost. We can't afford to pay staff, so we have a group of volunteers who take turns working the shifts we need to cover."

"That's really awesome. I guess you know I operate a shelter myself."

"Jake mentioned it. I'd love to have a facility someday that would allow us to care for our injured wildlife, but that takes a lot more money than can be scraped together with a bake sale."

It occurred to me that I should talk to Zak about making a donation to the shelter. He was always looking for worthwhile nonprofits to contribute to. I didn't want to say anything to Harmony until I had a chance to speak to him about it.

"So you focus on dogs and cats?" I asked.

"Mainly. We get a few other types of animals dropped off from time to time, and we try to take in whoever might show up at our door. One of the women who attends the same Tuesday morning coffee klatch I do does all the bookkeeping for us, which is nice because neither Chloe nor I are really into keeping track of all the little details that need to be attended to in order to maintain our nonprofit status."

"Yeah, it really is time-consuming."

My phone rang as Harmony turned into the parking lot that was shared by all the businesses on the main drag.

"I really should get this," I apologized.

"No problem. Do you need privacy?"

"No, stay. This should just take a moment." I clicked my phone on. "Hey, El. How's it going?"

I noticed Harmony frown when my jaw dropped open. "What do you mean he's dead? Who killed him?" I listened while Ellie explained that Levi had gone looking for the guy who had set fire to the lumberyard and run them off the road. He'd found his truck parked on a logging road, with a man's dead body in the driver's seat.

"How did Levi even know who to look for?" I asked.

"He didn't. He just went looking for a black truck. When he saw it on the side of the road he recognized it immediately."

"What did Salinger say?" I asked Ellie after she told me the man had been shot, but Levi didn't know who'd done it. When I insisted that she tell me everything that was going on, Ellie said Levi had freaked out when he found the man and left the scene of the crime. I frowned and bit my lip as I tried to figure out what to do. Ellie was hysterical, and if I knew Levi—and I did—he would insist that waiting to let someone else find the body would be the path of least resistance. Harmony offered me a look of sympathy as I massaged my temple with the fingers of my free hand.

"Okay, this is what I want you to do," I instructed. "I want you both to stay put in the house. No more sleuthing. I'll call Salinger to see if there's a way I can inform him of the location of the body without getting Levi thrown in jail.

"It'll be fine," I said, trying to comfort my hysterical friend. "I'll call you back after I talk to Salinger."

I shrugged in apology over the long conversation as Harmony patiently waited for me to complete my call.

"I know, and I love you too," I said to Ellie. "Now put Levi on the line."

After I got Levi to promise to stay put while I tried to deal with things I turned toward Harmony.

"Trouble at home?" she asked.

"That's putting it mildly." I briefly explained about my two best friends and the accident they'd been involved in the day before we arrived in Alaska. "I'm sorry, but I need to make another call."

"That's perfectly fine." Harmony smiled. "I think it's awesome that you have friends who you're so close to, and I completely understand. If something happened to Chloe, Jake, or anyone from the search and rescue team, I'd move heaven and earth to help them. Is there anything I can do?"

"Thanks for the offer, but no. I need to call Sheriff Salinger, and then I'll need to call Levi and Ellie back."

"Let's head over to Chloe's place," Harmony suggested. "You can make the calls from her office. It will certainly be warmer than sitting in the van. We can just switch things up a bit and have lunch first and then come back for the dress."

"Thanks." I sighed gratefully. "That sounds like a good plan."

Chloe's Corner reminded me a lot of Rosie's. It was warm and cozy, with a lot of antiques on the walls. There was a "locals" bulletin board prominently displayed that featured everything from flyers for babysitters wanted to announcements about the local darts tournament and the special on snow shovels the hardware store was having.

Harmony introduced me to Chloe, who was friendly and approachable. I could see that the two girls shared a relationship much like the one I had with Ellie. After taking our lunch orders Chloe showed me to her office, where I could use the phone in private. Luckily, Salinger was in and willing to take my call.

"So how's Alaska?" Salinger asked.

"Cold."

"I take it this isn't a social call?"

"I like a man who gets right to the point," I teased. "And no, this isn't a social call. I actually have information for you about Poke Blane. Or at least I think I do."

"Do tell. What information might that be?"

I could almost see Salinger yawning at what he assumed would be irrelevant information, given my considerable distance from the investigation.

"He's dead."

"What? How do you know that?" Salinger demanded.

"I have my sources. You'll find a black truck, along with a body, on the old logging road you catch just beyond the bridge. I don't know for certain it's the man you're looking for, but given the circumstance I'd be willing to bet it is."

"Because you're thousands of miles away I'm going to assume you didn't stumble upon this information by sheer coincidence," Salinger accused.

"Like I said, I have my sources."

"And is your source responsible for Mr. Poke's state of deadness?" Salinger asked.

"No. My source is completely innocent."

Salinger hesitated before continuing. "I see. I'll head over to check out this very helpful lead you've supplied me with. Please be sure to tell your source to keep his distance from the investigation from this point forward if he doesn't want to spend one or more nights in jail."

"I'll do that," I promised.

"So when are you going to be back in Ashton Falls?" Salinger asked.

"Why? Do you miss me?" I teased.

"Actually, it's been inconvenient for you to be gone at this particular time."

Aw, the guy really liked me.

"I'll be back in a couple of days," I informed him. "In the meantime, I'll call my source to tell him to stay put."

After speaking with both Ellie and Levi and getting their absolute promise to stay out of Salinger's way, I went back into the dining area of the restaurant to join Harmony and Chloe. There were only a few tables occupied, which wasn't all that surprising considering half of the businesses on Main Street had signs in the window stating they were closed for the season.

"Is everything okay?" Harmony asked when I joined her and Chloe at the table where they'd been chatting.

"I think so. Fortunately, I've developed a relationship with the local sheriff over the past year, so he tends to give me the benefit of the doubt in most circumstances."

"I hope your friend appreciates everything you do for him," Harmony said.

"He does. Levi is a great guy. We've been best friends since kindergarten. He's really more like a brother than just a friend and I love him dearly, but he can be a hothead, which gets him into trouble at times."

"Wyatt's like that," Harmony informed me. "He's the sweetest guy in the world, but he tends to act on his emotions, and that's gotten him into trouble on more than one occasion."

"Actually, Wyatt did remind me of Levi when I first met him," I commented. "The members of the team seem to get along really well, but they all seem so different in terms of personality."

"Yeah, I guess they are," Harmony acknowledged, "which is probably what makes us such a good team. We complement one another."

I turned to look at Chloe. "Harmony tells me that you volunteer at the local animal shelter."

"I do, and I love it. Harm and I both donate a lot of time to the shelter, but it's very rewarding."

"You must be pretty busy between doing your volunteer work and running this business."

Chloe shrugged. "It's hard to juggle everything during the summer, but the coffee shop is slow during the winter, so I have quite a bit of free time. By the way," Chloe turned and looked at Harmony, "Harley is back in town. He was asking about you."

"Harley?" I asked.

"Harley Medford is the man who owns the land where the shelter is located. He has a thing for Harmony, so he was happy to help out when she asked him to donate the building."

"He doesn't have a thing for me," Harmony argued.

Chloe looked directly at me. "Trust me, the man is smitten. And he's been smitten ever since Harmony punched him in the second grade for spilling his soda down the front of her new jacket."

I laughed. "Sounds like my kind of romance."

"There's no romance," Harmony insisted. "Harley had a building he wasn't using, I asked him if we could use it, and he agreed. There's never been anything more to it than that."

"Smitten," Chloe mouthed silently.

"Can we stop talking about romances that don't exist and change the subject?" Harmony gave Chloe a best-friend glance. Chloe just grinned.

"I called over to the boutique while you were on the phone and Erin said she had a couple of dresses she thinks you'll love," Harmony informed me. "I told her we'd be by after we eat, if that's still okay."

"Sounds great. I noticed a lot of the shops on Main Street have signs announcing that they're closed for the season."

"The stores that close tend to be geared toward summer visitors," Harmony said. "The ones that cater to the residents of Moosehead—the grocery store, the hardware store, the pharmacy, the bookstore, and a few of the clothing stores—stay open year-round. The town can seem pretty isolated in the winter, but the local hangouts provide a feeling of community. Neverland can get pretty busy if there's a darts tournament going on, and Chloe hosts several different groups."

"Groups?" I asked.

"Book clubs, event committees, women's groups, and bible studies, among others," Chloe informed me. "There aren't a lot of entertainment options in the area, so people tend to gather and eat."

"There's a group that's trying to raise funds to bring in a real movie theater," Harmony informed me. "We currently use the high school gym to show movies, but we don't have the means to show first-run films."

"We don't have a movie theater either," I commented. "But there's a nice one in Bryton Lake, which is only thirty minutes away."

Chloe looked up as a group of six men walked into the restaurant and sat down at a large table in the corner.

"Looks like I have customers," Chloe announced. "It was nice meeting you, Zoe. Come back by before you leave if you get a chance."

"I will."

After lunch I met Harmony's friend Erin and found a perfect dress for the party. Erin was one of those people who at first glance seems like a square peg trying to fit into a round hole, but upon further exposure you realize she's just as round as everyone else.

On one hand, she was both gorgeous and glamorous. In spite of the fact that the snow outside her door could be measured in feet, she wore a short skirt with a tight sweater and three-inch heels. Her silky blond hair had been expertly cut to accentuate her flawless skin and light blue eyes, her makeup applied as perfectly as if it had been done by a professional. She looked like someone you'd find working in a boutique on Rodeo Drive in Beverly Hills rather than the owner of a small boutique in Moosehead, Alaska.

Once you began to talk to her, however, you realized she was as down-to-earth and friendly as Harmony and Chloe. She volunteered at the shelter too, and had two cats of her own at home. I could see that Harmony, Chloe, and Erin were all close friends who had known each other for a number of years.

Erin and I spoke for a few minutes before she asked me some questions about color preferences and whatnot and then presented me with the perfect dress. And when I say perfect I mean *perfect*. It fit me like a glove in spite of my petite frame, and the color was absolutely spot-on to show off my natural coloring.

After thanking Erin for her help, Harmony and I headed back to the tavern to check on the status of the investigation into Carter Christianson, his photos, and his murder. I knew Zak had planned to head over there once he'd returned from his walk with Marty, so I'd arranged to meet him there. The tavern was open at four on Tuesdays, so Jake's cook, Serge, was on-site to get things prepped for the evening meals.

"How were your days off?" Harmony asked Serge as she kissed the tattooed man with the bald head on the cheek.

"Met up with my new gal and we had a right nice time." Serge winked.

"Did you go out?" she asked.

"Actually, we stayed in." He winked again.

"You are so bad." Harmony slapped him on the arm. "You remember Zoe?"

"I do. How's Sitka doing?"

"He's doing great. He certainly doesn't need me to be here any longer, but I thought I'd stay for the party tomorrow night."

"Just gonna be a lot of drunks making a lot of racket in order to celebrate the fact that one minute has passed since before they started caterwauling like there was no tomorrow."

"Ignore Serge," Harmony advised. "He just likes to complain. What's the special tonight?"

"Grilled halibut fillets with chipotle Béarnaise sauce."

"Sounds fantastic," I commented, "but I thought you just did sandwiches and soups."

"Mostly we do just serve a bar-type menu, but Serge likes to cook, so he has a special every now and then. Herbed potatoes?"

"Garlic mashed with broccoli and carrots."

Suddenly I found myself wishing I hadn't had such a big lunch.

"Looks like the guys are hard at it," Harmony observed as she glanced at Zak, Jake, and Landon sitting at a table with laptops in front of each of them. They were so intent on their tasks that I doubted they'd even heard us come in.

"Yup. Seems like they might have found something. They seemed pretty excited about something a little while ago."

Harmony and I decided to go over to check it out. We hated to interrupt, but if they'd found something that would shed light on either death we wanted to know what it was.

"How is it going?" I asked the group.

Zak looked up and smiled at me. "We've made some progress. Pull up a chair. Both of you."

Harmony and I did as instructed. Charlie, who had been with Zak all morning, happily climbed into my lap.

"So what did you find?" I asked the guys, who had stopped what they were doing when Harmony and I approached.

"I think we've narrowed down the suspect list a bit," Jake stated. "At the very least, we have new information on each of our suspects."

"Like what?" Harmony asked.

"If we operate under the assumption that of the fourteen people locked inside the inn that night, Colin didn't kill himself, Zoe and I didn't do it, and Marty and Mary are innocent based on the fact that they're known and liked in the community, we have nine suspects," Zak started. "Ethel is too old and Bart is too short, which leaves us with seven suspects. We decided to divide up the list. I've been looking for information regarding Drake Rutherford and Liza Aldren. Landon took Grover Wood and Turner Hawthorn, and Jake took Jerid Richardson and Barry and Stella Ward."

"And?" Harmony prodded as Whiskey jumped up onto the table and lay down smack dab in the middle.

"And I think we've narrowed it down a bit," Zak answered. "I'll start."

I settled in and waited for Zak to begin his summary. He's so sexy when he does the brain thing. I would have no idea where to even start to dig up dirt on someone, but Zak was a wiz at making his way around the Internet highway.

"Drake Rutherford seems to be at the inn to do exactly what he says he's doing: writing his next book. It seems his last book didn't do as well as his publisher hoped, so there's a lot of pressure on him to do really well with this one. The only photo of Drake in the case Zoe found was one of him in the common area of the inn, talking to Ethel and Grover. It's hard to know for certain, but I'd say we can take him off the list unless new information comes to light."

Everyone indicated that they agreed.

"As for Liza Aldren, I've looked into her past travel and I'll admit it seems odd that she's here. I know she said she's here to ski, but her travel history shows that she normally skis in areas that have great mountains but also have five-star resorts. The only explanation I can come up with as to why she might be in Moosehead is Jerid Richardson. The two have been photographed together on several occasions in the past year, so if I had to guess, I'd say she followed him here. Jerid is after extreme conditions over luxury, so it actually makes sense that he would come to a place like Moosehead."

"I agree," Jake jumped in. "In the past few years Jerid has tackled some increasingly difficult mountains. Dani has told me on more than one occasion that Jerid intentionally looked for the most difficult way down the mountain. If you ask me, the guy is an adrenaline junkie."

"Okay, so we can speculate as to why Jerid and Liza might be here, but does that make them innocent?" I asked.

Jake looked at me. "Not at all. However, we haven't found anything suspect either. I looked at the photos. There was one taken at a community meal and another as a few of the residents sat around a card table, but nothing that seemed at all suspicious."

"So that leaves Turner, Barry and Stella, and Grover," I summarized.

"Barry and Stella seem to be what they say they are on the surface," Jake continued. "They were married a few days before arriving in Moosehead in a big ceremony with family and friends in attendance after a yearlong engagement. The only thing that's odd is that they didn't make their reservation at the inn until a few days before the wedding."

"I'm surprised Marty and Mary had a room for them on such short notice," Harmony commented.

"I called them and they said they'd had a last-minute cancellation because one of their guests was in an auto accident."

"You'd think that if they'd been engaged for a year they would have made their honeymoon plans months ago," I added.

"It would seem," Jake agreed.

"I wouldn't take them off the list just yet," Harmony said. "There's something that feels off about the whole thing."

"I agree," I added. "What's up with Turner and Grover?"

"Turner Hawthorn just got out of prison and Grover Wood doesn't exist," Landon provided.

"What do you mean Grover Wood doesn't exist?" I asked.

"I mean there's no trace of him," Landon clarified. "The man at the inn is obviously using a fake identity."

"Then it has to be him," Harmony announced.

"Not necessarily," Landon cautioned. "Just because he was using a fake name doesn't mean he's a killer."

"Yeah, but he isn't just lying about his name but also his reason for being here. He obviously isn't a geologist."

"No," Landon said, "he doesn't appear to be."

"We might not be able to prove he did it quite yet, but he seems to be the most likely suspect we have so far," Jake added.

"What about Turner?" I asked. "What was he in prison for?"

"Murder in the first degree. But here's the odd thing: he was released after serving only a year. Who gets released after only a year if they've been convicted of first-degree murder?"

"Good question," I said. "So what now? We haven't narrowed things down much."

"I thought you and I could go back to the Inn and try to work up conversations with everyone," Zak suggested. "We can ask Barry and Stella about their wedding and honeymoon plans, and maybe they'll offer a perfectly logical explanation as to why they made a last-minute reservation. We can also chat with Liza, bringing up the fact that Moosehead doesn't seem like one of her usual haunts."

"How do we handle Turner and Grover?" I wondered. "It's not like we can come right out and ask Turner how he managed to get out of prison so early, and Grover has checked out."

"He checked out?" Zak asked.

"Yeah; I thought you knew. Mary told me that he checked out this morning. He originally was supposed to stay through January, but he told Mary that his work got wrapped up early so he was leaving right away."

"That really does make him sound guilty," Harmony added.

"Yeah." Zak frowned. "It does. But I think we would be remiss to stop looking just because it appears we have a suspect. I think we should still talk to the others."

"The tavern is open tonight, so Harmony and I will be working," Jake informed us. "Landon's going to continue to dig, and Jordan said she'll come over when she finishes her shift at the clinic."

"And Dani and Wyatt?" I asked.

"Dani had a date with Jerid," Jake answered.

"Which should thrill Liza if she did follow him here," I commented.

"It might make her more open to chatting if you lend a sympathetic ear," Harmony reminded me.

"And Wyatt?" I asked.

"I haven't spoken to him since the rescue last night and he isn't answering his cell," Jake said.

No one else had spoken to him either.

"Okay." I stood up. "Zak and I will go do our thing and you guys do yours and we'll meet up tomorrow to compare notes."

Chapter 12

Zak and I returned to the inn for dinner, which worked out well because everyone who was currently staying there came down for the evening meal with the exception of Jerid, who was out with Dani. This was actually the first time Zak and I had eaten the last meal of the day at the inn. Everyone gathered in the living room to have a drink and discuss their day while they waited for the food to be served.

"So how are you enjoying Moosehead?" I asked Stella as I joined her where she stood in front of the fire.

"Honestly, I can't wait to get home and enjoy some tepid weather. I'm not really a huge fan of the cold."

"And yet you chose to go to Alaska for your honeymoon?" I probed.

"Trust me; it wasn't my idea. I had reservations for us to spend two weeks in tropical Tahiti, but then Barry's uncle decided to surprise us with the ski trip. Barry loves to ski, so I guess I can see how he got the idea to send us here, but I wasn't at all happy with the change. I wanted to politely decline the gift, but Barry didn't want to hurt his uncle's feelings."

I had to admit I felt sorry for Stella. A honeymoon was a once-in-a-lifetime event that should be enjoyed by both parties in the relationship.

"I guess you can still go to Tahiti," I sympathized. "Maybe for your first anniversary?"

"If we *have* a first anniversary. I've been thinking a lot about spending my life with a man who cares more about not hurting his uncle's feelings than he does about making his wife happy. The first few days we were here I really tried to make the best of it, but the colder I got and the more snow that fell the more irritated I became. I would have left by now, but the tickets for our flight home aren't the kind you can change without paying a huge fee."

"I'm sorry to hear you haven't been enjoying your trip. I understand the room you're staying in just became available a few days before you arrived. It seems odd that Barry's uncle would book the trip when he couldn't be certain there'd be a room for you to stay in."

"Barry's uncle is one of those men who gets his own way. I'm sure he would have figured something out if the inn didn't end up with a vacancy. If you ask me, the man intentionally gave us a gift he knew I'd hate. I don't think the guy really likes me, and while I don't know for certain he knew about the trip I'd planned, I really wouldn't put it past him to use the ski trip as a ploy to create conflict in our relationship."

"You really think he would do that?" I asked.

"I know he would." Stella looked around the room. She frowned at her new husband. "I'm going to get another drink before dinner's served. It's been nice talking to you."

"Nice talking to you too."

I felt bad for the woman; I certainly wouldn't want to be married to a man who didn't put my feelings ahead of those of an uncle when it came to our honeymoon. I looked around the room for Zak, who was speaking to Liza. I tried not to be jealous over the fact that Liza touched Zak's chest every time she laughed, which was often. I was about to make my way to join them when Turner walked up with a scotch bottle.

"Refill?" he asked.

"No, thank you. I'll wait to have wine with dinner. Are you enjoying your trip so far?"

The man shrugged. "It's okay. I've certainly spent time in worse places."

I tried to figure out a way to work his stay in prison into the conversation but was coming up blank.

"Have you stayed here before?" I asked.

"No. First time."

"We were here last year over Christmas only there wasn't as much snow," I lied, using Jake's comment about the snow load. "Where did you spend your holiday last year?"

"In prison."

Okay; I wasn't expecting that to be quite so easy.

"I guess if I had to choose this would be better," Turner commented.

"Well, I would think so. Were you in prison long?" I asked.

"That depends on how you define long. I think I'm going to go grab one of those crab cakes before they're all gone. I'm taking the bottle, so just let me know if you change your mind about a refill."

To be honest, I wasn't certain what to think about what I'd learned from either of our suspects. Both had ended the conversation we were having somewhat abruptly, but neither had said anything incriminating either. I suppose I could see how they would be anxious to leave; I'd steered both toward subjects they might prefer not to discuss.

"So are you here with anyone?" Zak teased as he walked across the room to join me.

"Apparently not," I teased back. "How was your conversation with our resident supermodel?"

"Informative. It appears she's in Moosehead because of a deal that was worked out between her publicist and Jerid's manager."

"Deal? What kind of a deal?"

"They arranged for Jerid and Liza to hang out and be seen together. She thinks the guy is a creep, but she shared that she's gotten some higher-paying gigs since the tabloids have started following them around."

"So they're pretending to have a relationship in order to get free publicity?"

"Apparently. Liza is sick of the whole thing, but I guess she's lost some big jobs lately because even though she's only thirty, that's considered old to be a model. Hooking up with a young daredevil like Jerid is helping her to redefine her image as a young and wild trendsetter. She said she resisted the idea at first, but it really seems to be working."

"But why would anyone think they'd be photographed together in Moosehead? I doubt there are paparazzi hanging out in the streets," I pointed out.

"Liza said they were originally supposed to go to a resort in Colorado, but Jerid refused because, according to him, the mountain wasn't challenging enough. Initially, Liza refused to come to Moosehead, viewing it as a total waste of her time, but her publicist convinced her to make the trip with the promise that there would be photos leaked of the daredevil couple. The fact that they seemed to be hiding out in this little town added to the mystery of it all. According to Liza, several tabloids have already picked up the story of their romantic interlude off the grid."

"So the publicist must have sent a photographer. Does Liza know who?"

"She said she didn't know who took the photos, but I suspect she's lying."

"Okay, so we know why Liza and Jerid are here and the newlyweds appear to be just that, so where does it leave us?" I asked.

"Unless we can prove it's either Turner or Grover, we're seriously short on suspects," Zak confirmed.

After dinner Zak and I went up to our room. I can't say we were any closer to finding the killer in spite of the fact that we had actually gotten quite a few of our questions answered. Zak also had had a conversation with Turner Hawthorn, who'd let slip that the reason he was released from prison after only a year was that new evidence had come to light that put his guilt in serious doubt. Rather than retry him for a crime he probably hadn't committed, a deal had been worked out to release him with time served. Turner could have insisted on a new trial in order to prove his innocence, but he told Zak he just wanted to put the whole thing behind him and get on with his life. Zak told me that he was fairly certain the man was actually guilty and the new evidence was simply a lucky break.

So, I asked myself as I waited for Zak to finish up some e-mails, where exactly did that leave us? We had no way of speaking to Grover Wood, or whatever his real name was. I suppose the fact that he checked in using an alias and left early should put him at the top of the suspect list.

I was about to take a shower when my cell rang. It was Salinger. I held my breath as I answered the call because I was half-expecting him to tell me that he'd thought about it and decided to arrest Levi for leaving the scene of a crime or, worse yet, that he'd called to say he'd arrested him for murder.

"Salinger," I said.

"Donovan."

"You have news?" I prompted.

"I do. Are you able to speak freely?"

Uh-oh. This didn't sound good.

"Yeah, I can talk," I answered. "What's up?"

"I wanted to let you know that the state police made an arrest in Poke Blane's death."

"It's not Levi?"

"No, it's not Levi." Salinger chuckled. "It turns out Poke Blane was not only a security guard at the prison, he was a dirty security guard who passed information back and forth between the prisoners and people on the outside for a price. They had reason to believe Poke was being squeezed from the inside, which is why he quit his job. The guys from the state brought Buck Stevenson in for questioning, and he admitted to having knowledge of Blane's activities during the time he was in prison. He's working with the police to try to track down everyone involved."

"And the fire at his place?" I wondered.

"Buck believes it was a warning that he would be best served by keeping what he knew to himself. It seems Blane helped some pretty dangerous men orchestrate some pretty heinous crimes while they were incarcerated."

"So why run Levi and Ellie off the road?" I wondered.

"I'm afraid the only man who can tell us that for certain is dead."

Salinger had a point. It made no sense for Blane to have gone after Levi and Ellie. I suppose if he had a reason for doing so, we'd never know what it was.

"So do you know who killed Blane?"

"Not yet, but the guys from the state are working a couple of leads. I do have news of another nature, however."

"Such as?" I looked down at Charlie, who had wandered over and put his paw on my foot.

"When you called to tell me the location of the truck and our dead arsonist, I thought it odd."

"Odd why?" I asked.

"Because of all the snow we've had. Most of the time those old logging roads are impassable during the winter."

I realized Salinger had a good point. "That's true. So how did Poke get his truck up the road?"

"It had been plowed."

I frowned. "Who plowed it?"

"That's the very question I asked myself, so after I had the body removed and the truck towed I looked around a bit. I noticed that one of the old summer cabins had smoke coming from the chimney. You'll never guess what I found when I went to investigate."

"The meth lab," I realized.

Last summer, while the gang and I were in Maui, Jeremy Fisher, my assistant at the Zoo, had had a problem with dead squirrels and sick dogs. After some investigation we'd found that the groundwater in the affected area was contaminated with what looked to be waste associated with a meth lab. The waste had been cleaned up and the threat to the animals removed, but Salinger never had been able to find the source of the material.

"Very good." Salinger sounded impressed. "How did you know?"

"I didn't, but when you mentioned the plowed road the meth lab popped into my head. Those cabins are a long way away from the site where we found the contaminated water," I added.

"Apparently, the chemistry student who'd been cooking the stuff was an environmentalist. He didn't want to have happen exactly what did happen, so he was disposing of the waste in an abandoned septic tank. What he didn't know was that the tank had a leak."

"So you were able to arrest him?" I clarified.

"We got all four men who were on site at the time of the bust and we have a lead on a couple of others. I have a feeling we might be able to close this case."

"I'm glad it worked out. Do you think Blane Poke's presence on that particular road had anything to do with the lab?"

"Probably not. I think the road simply provided a convenient place for him to meet whomever it was who killed him."

After I hung up the phone with Salinger I had to shake my head at the strange twist that had allowed Salinger to finally solve the case of the meth lab while investigating a seemingly unrelated murder.

"That was Salinger," I told Zak, who was still working at the computer.

"Hmm," Zak replied.

"They've arrested Levi for his murder," I announced, in an effort to see whether Zak was even listening to me.

No response.

"Salinger says he'll get the death penalty."

"That's nice." Zak frowned at something on the screen in front of him.

"Which is really a drag, considering I'm currently pregnant with his baby."

Zak stopped typing and looked at me. "What?"

"Have you heard anything I've said?"

"I heard that last part."

I returned my phone to the bedside table and sat down on the edge. "I'm trying to tell you that the state police took over the Poke Blane murder investigation."

Zak frowned. "Does he know why?"

I let out a long breath. "I've already explained all of this."

"Sorry. When I'm writing code I tend to zone out."

"Yeah. I understand. I just think it's odd that . . ."

I was interrupted by the ringing of my phone. "It's my mom," I announced.

"Tell her hi for me." Zak went back to his task.

"Hey, Mom, what's up?" I answered.

"I was wondering if you had a minute to talk."

"Sure; what's on your mind?"

"Wedding plans."

"You want to talk about the wedding now?"

"If you have a few minutes."

I tried not to let a deep sigh slip out. I loved having my mom in my life, and it meant so much to me that she wanted to be involved with my wedding, but honestly, bridal bouquets and reception venues were the last thing I wanted to talk about just then.

"Of course I have a minute," I said diplomatically. "What's on your mind?"

An hour later, I was finally wrapping up what had turned into a marathon conversation. "Yes, Mom, I'll ask him."

Zak looked up at me and I shrugged.

"Yes, soon. Good night now."

I sighed as I finally was able to hang up the phone. "That was my mother."

"Yes, you already mentioned that." Zak smiled. "What did she want?"

"You can't figure that out based on my end of the conversation?" I said irritably.

"Sorry; I returned to my tunnel vision as soon as you started talking."

"She wanted to talk about the wedding," I informed him. "I tried to tell her that we'd start thinking about it after the new year, but she kept insisting that these things take time and we really shouldn't wait too long to start making plans. I just don't get where this is coming from. When she married Dad last summer she didn't even want to have a reception."

"Which you insisted on," Zak pointed out.

"I did. But she wanted to keep it small."

"Which you didn't."

"Maybe not, but I guess I expected that she more than most would understand my need to maintain a certain level of sanity throughout this process."

"And she's being insane?" Zak asked.

"Completely insane." I groaned. "She wants to take me dress shopping when we get home."

Zak gave me one of his adorable half grins. "I'm not an expert at planning weddings, but dress shopping sounds like a reasonable idea."

"In *Paris*. The woman wants to go shopping in *Paris*. Like I can take time off work to hop over to the continent on a whim."

"You came to Alaska on a whim," Zak said.

"That was entirely different. There's no way I'm going to fly halfway around the world to buy a dress. Does Amazon have wedding dresses? 'Cause if they do I'm a Prime member. Free shipping."

Zak laughed out loud. "You can't seriously be thinking about buying a wedding gown over the Internet."

"Why not? It's both time- and cost-effective."

Zak got up and walked across the room. He pulled me into his arms and held me to his chest. "Don't worry about the dress. I'm sure your mom will understand that you aren't the Paris type once she thinks about it. Was there anything else?"

"Our honeymoon."

"She doesn't want to come, does she?" Zak tried for a light tone of voice.

"No." I grinned. "She doesn't want to come. But she spoke to Clara, who offered us the use of her estate in Tuscany."

Clara Field was a friend of my mom's who'd helped us out by bidding on Zak at the bachelor auction the previous month.

"Tuscany is nice," Zak offered.

"I'm sure it is, but it isn't exactly what I had in mind."

Zak took my hand and led me over to the small sofa that was situated in front of the fire. He continued to hold my hand as he asked, "What exactly *did* you have in mind?"

"I don't know. Somewhere different from Tuscany. Clara was so nice to us, though, so I don't want to hurt her feelings."

"Clara doesn't seem the type to get her feelings hurt easily," Zak pointed out.

"Yeah," I acknowledged. "I guess that's true."

"You know . . ." Zak said in a tone I'd come to recognize as his cautious voice, which he used when he thought I might go ballistic over some little thing. "The best way to keep others from trying to control our wedding is to decide what it is we want and then inform everyone that the decisions have been made and are nonnegotiable. Your mom is just excited that we're getting married; I'm sure she doesn't mean to steamroll you. My mom, on the other hand, is going to eat us alive if she sees even a tiny in."

Zak hadn't as of yet informed his mom of our impending nuptials. He wanted us to have our plans in place before she found out.

"I guess we should start thinking about things," I acknowledged.

"Like a date?" Zak asked hopefully.

"Yeah, like a date. Scooter and Alex both want to be in the wedding, and if there's one thing I *do* know it's that I want them there, so I guess we should look at doing it during the summer, when they're off school. I thought Charlie and Bella could be the ring bearers and Scooter and Alex could walk them down the aisle."

"I love that idea." Zak kissed me gently on the lips. "Look at us; we made a decision."

I laughed. "Yeah, only a couple million more to go."

"The first one is the hardest," Zak explained. "So do you have a preference as far as which summer month we get married in?"

"My parents just got married in August, so I think of that as their month, and it can still be cold in June and I'd like to have the ceremony on the beach, so July. I think the end of July would work well."

Zak pulled out his cell and looked at the calendar. "How about the twenty-fifth? That's the last Saturday of the month."

"Yeah, I like that. July twenty-fifth."

"See? That wasn't so hard. We know we're getting married on the beach on July twenty-fifth, and Charlie, Bella, Scooter, and Alex are going to walk the rings down the aisle. We just need a reception site, a maid of honor, and a best man and we'll pretty much be set."

"Levi and Ellie?"

"That sounds perfect. And the reception?"

I could tell Zak was limping me along, but we did seem to be making some progress, so I let him.

"I really do want to keep it manageable. I was thinking of just having it at your house."

"Our house," Zak corrected. "And that sounds perfect."

"Jeremy can do the music," I added, "and I'm sure between Ellie and Rosie they can plan the food. We'll hire servers for the day of the ceremony, though, so they can relax and enjoy the party. I know Hazel and Phyllis will want to do the flowers, and I want my dad to walk me down the aisle. Actually," I corrected, "I'd like Mom, Dad, and Harper all to walk me down the aisle."

"Wow, two minutes and we're pretty much planned." Zak grinned. "Now, how about the honeymoon?"

"I'm all planned out. How about we sleep on it?"

"I could sleep." Zak lifted me up and carried me to the bed. "Eventually."

Chapter 13

Wednesday, December 31

Zak was out dogsledding with Marty and we weren't expected to show up at Neverland until the party that evening, so I did what any woman left on her own for a few hours would do: I went shoe shopping. I'd been thinking about a pair I'd seen in Erin's boutique when I'd been there shopping with Harmony, but I'd decided not to splurge on them at the time. You know what they say about hindsight? Suffice it to say that upon further reflection, I'd decided I really did *need* to have them, despite the fact that they were going to cost me a week's salary.

Harmony was busy getting the tavern ready for the New Year's Eve party, so I called the only taxi service in Moosehead: a guy named Joe with a beat-up SUV. Luckily, Erin didn't mind me bringing Charlie along because I really hated to leave him alone.

"I had a feeling you'd be back." Erin greeted.

"Oh, and why is that?"

"I recognized the lust in your eyes when you spied those shoes. They really are exceptional. I'm almost sold out of them, but you have such tiny feet and I still have the size fives."

I sat down on a small lounge she provided for patrons to use when trying on shoes. This might seem odd, but I actually own very few pairs of high heels. My lifestyle doesn't dictate a need for such luxuries, but I had a killer dress for the party and paired with these shoes . . . Let's just say that if Zak hadn't already proposed he surely would have that night.

Erin answered the store phone while I tried on the shoes and walked around the carpeted room. I was at least three inches taller with the spiky heeled leg extenders. It would be nice to look Zak in the face rather than the middle of the chest, which is what I usually did when we danced.

"I'm sorry; that was Ethel Montros checking on the clothes she left for alteration," Erin apologized.

"I wasn't aware you offered alteration services."

"I don't. At least not generally. But Ethel is always picking up new clothes when she travels and then deciding when she gets back to Moosehead that they don't fit quite right. She offered me a ridiculous amount of money to do some easy alterations, so I figured what the heck. She's leaving for Prague next week and wants to be sure they're ready."

"She certainly gets around for someone of her age and physical limitations."

"Don't let her fool you," Erin warned. "Ethel is a strong gal, and I believe she's quite a bit younger than she lets on."

"Younger? I've heard about people using tons of makeup and lying about their age to seem younger, but why would you lie about your age in an attempt to seem older?"

"If you want my opinion, I think she likes the attention that comes with being old and feeble."

I frowned. "I thought Mary said she was arthritic."

"I don't think so. I've personally seen her open a jar most men couldn't have opened. Besides, I've helped her to change in and out of the outfits I'm altering. The woman doesn't have the body of an eighty-year-old, and I think the gray hair is a wig."

"But her face and hands?"

"Makeup. Professionally applied makeup. Listen, if you're going back to the inn would you mind taking this pair of pants with you? Ethel specifically asked that they be ready today."

"Sure, no problem. I arranged for Joe to come back to get Charlie and me in half an hour, if that will work."

"That will be perfect."

The first thing I did after Charlie and I got back to the inn was review the photos I'd found in the dead reporter's room. While it was true that there were photos of each of the inn's guests, I hadn't noted before that Ethel was in *all* of them. Could it be that Carter had been taking photos of Ethel all along, and that the other guests just happened to end up in the shots?

I looked at the photos taken from locations other than the inn. They'd all been taken in large cities and all contained a large number of people, but what I hadn't noticed before was that a woman with long black hair who appeared to be about fifty was in quite a few of the shots. I held up the best photo I could find of that woman and the best I could find of Ethel and compared them.

The woman with the black hair and Ethel seemed to be of similar build and height, although it was hard to tell for certain because there were no photos of them standing next to each other. Ethel had short gray hair and a plethora of bags and wrinkles, whereas the woman with the dark hair had a clear complexion with only a few fine lines. They had a similarly shaped face, but the woman with the black hair was wearing sunglasses in every photo, so I couldn't get a look at her eyes.

If the woman with the black hair and Ethel were the same person, Ethel had to be some sort of master of disguise. Even though I was looking for proof that the two were actually the same, my eyes couldn't get past the more than thirty-year age difference.

I decided to head over to Ethel's room. If she wasn't old and feeble like she wanted everyone to believe, she really should have been added to the suspect list. We hadn't looked into her background as we had the others because we didn't believe she had the physical ability to strangle our visiting reporter.

"Yes?" Ethel responded when I knocked on her door.

"It's Zoe Donovan. I was in town buying shoes when you called about your alterations," I explained through the still-closed door. "I have the pants you wanted delivered today."

"I'm afraid you've caught me at a bad time. I'm not dressed to receive visitors. Can you please just leave the pants with Mary and I'll get them from her later?"

"Uh, sure."

I hated to lose my chance to speak to the woman, but I had no reason to demand that she open the door. I headed downstairs in search of the inn's owner.

"Erin from the boutique gave these to me to deliver to Ethel, but she claims to be indisposed," I explained to Mary, who I located in the laundry room.

"You can just set them on the counter. I'll be sure she gets them."

"I remember you said Ethel keeps a room in the inn on an annual basis. How long has she been a resident here?" I asked as casually as I could muster.

Mary stopped folding the towel in her hand as she thought about it. "I guess almost three years now. Of course, she's away more often than she's in town. I'm grateful for the steady income from her room, but it seems like a waste of money to me to keep a room when she's rarely here."

"Do you know how old she is?"

Mary screwed up her face. "I don't believe it's ever come up. She looks to be in her eighties."

"Erin seems to think she might be younger than she seems."

"I doubt it. She spends a lot of time in her room due to her various health issues and she certainly has the look of a woman well into her senior years."

I picked up a towel and started folding it. I figured I might as well pitch in as long as I was bending Mary's ear. Besides, she looked grateful for the help. It seemed that she took care of most of the chores around the inn while Marty was off with the dogs.

"Running an inn is really a lot of work," I said, trying for my most sympathetic tone.

Mary arched her back. "It really is. More than I anticipated when we decided to make the move."

"And you don't have help?"

"We have a girl who comes in to help with the cleaning and whatnot during the summer, but it doesn't make sense from a financial standpoint to pay someone from town during the winter. It'll get easier once things slow down a bit."

Mary looked up as someone came into the room behind me. I turned to see it was Ethel, looking as old and frail as ever. She walked across the room and picked up the bag.

"I'm going out for a while," she announced. "I could use some fresh towels, if you get a chance."

"I'll bring some up before you return. Have a nice time in town," Mary said as the woman turned and walked slowly away.

If Erin was correct and Ethel wasn't really old and physically challenged, it must take a tremendous amount of self-discipline to walk so slowly.

"I can take the towels up," I offered. "I was going to head up to my room to make a few phone calls anyway. It'll save you the trip up four flights of stairs."

Mary hesitated.

"It's really not a problem," I encouraged.

"I guess it would be okay. Just toss the old towels into the hall outside my room and I'll pick them up later."

"Will I need a key?" I asked.

Mary handed me a shiny gold key. "Just hang on to it until you come back down and then you can hang it on this hook." Mary pointed to a hook near the supply closet.

"Okay, no problem. I can just bring the soiled towels down as well after I make my calls."

"Aren't you so sweet and thoughtful?"

I wasn't sure my true intention could be described as sweet and thoughtful, but I didn't say as much.

I have to admit I felt a little guilty letting myself into Ethel's room with the towels. I hung them on the rack in the bathroom and tossed the soiled towels into the hall before I began looking around. The room was neat and tidy, and there was nothing on the surface to indicate that anyone other than an old lady lived there. I peeked into the bathroom cabinet, cracked open a couple of the dresser drawers, and rifled through the nightstand next to the bed. If Ethel really was a younger woman who, for reasons known only to her, made herself up to look old, she was hiding the evidence quite well.

In less than twenty minutes I would look back on my decision to search the closet as one of the worst I'd made in quite some time. It seemed like a logical place to hide cosmetics, wigs, or the other paraphernalia one would need to pull off such a ruse. I thumbed through the clothes hanging on the rack, peeked into a few of the shoe boxes lined up on the floor, and searched the wall for a removable panel or door. After quite a lot of time spent searching for the clue that seemed not to want to be found I realized the carpet in the corner of the closet was pulled slightly away from the door.

I leaned in and pulled the carpet back. Beneath the carpet was the trap door I'd been looking for. It was a small compartment with a smaller metal box inside. I pulled it out, hoping it wasn't locked. I opened the lid and gasped when I saw what was inside.

"What are you doing in here?" I heard a voice behind me.

I realized that only my backside sticking out of the closet was visible from the doorway, so I quickly replaced the box and covered it with the carpet. I backed out of the closet and looked at the woman, whose eyes suddenly conveyed her real age.

"Sorry," I mumbled as I stood up. "I dropped my contact lens and was looking for it."

"You dropped your contact inside my closet?"

"Mary asked me to bring up the towels, and while I was here I decided to make sure the pants I'd delivered had been hung from the heels, as Erin instructed."

Okay, I realize my explanation was the lamest in the history of all explanations, but I couldn't think of a single thing to say that might actually make sense. Based on the way Ethel's hand tightened on the small gun I just realized she was holding, I could see she wasn't buying my attempt at an excuse.

"I knew you were going to be trouble the minute you arrived," Ethel spat. "Little Miss Nosy Body, getting in everyone's business."

"So? I might be nosy, but at least I'm not a killer pretending to be an old woman."

Smooth, Zoe. Show her all your cards before she even places a wager.

Ethel waved the gun in my direction. "I guess you leave me no option."

"You're going to shoot me?" I paled.

"Eventually. For now, you're coming with me."

"Coming with you? Coming where?"

"You'll see. Now get a move on. My driver is waiting."

I thought about screaming, but then Mary would come running, and I didn't want her getting involved. Unless she was already involved? It seemed odd that the woman could live on the premises for so long without tipping her hand to the person who made her meals and cleaned her room.

"Does Mary know who you really are?" I asked.

"No. Do you?"

"No. Not really," I admitted.

I was grateful I'd dropped Charlie off in my room before coming to snoop around in Ethel's room; I'd hate for him to have gotten hurt due to my less than well-conceived plan.

"We're going to walk out of here without alerting anyone that there's a problem," Ethel informed me. "If you make a sound or say anything that might cause anyone who's currently at the inn to become suspicious, I'll shoot them and it will be your fault. Do you understand?"

"I understand."

Luckily—or perhaps unluckily; I wasn't certain at that point—Mary was elsewhere when we made our way down the stairs and out the front door. I slid into the limo that was waiting, just ahead of Ethel. Once we were settled the driver took off without having to be told where to go.

"Where are we going?" I asked.

"It doesn't matter; you won't be completing the trip anyway. You know I can't let you live."

"But why?" I tried to act shocked. "I won't tell anyone what I know."

The woman rolled her eyes.

"Really. I'm extremely good at keeping secrets. Ask anyone."

"If you think I'm going to fall for that you're wrong. I don't know what you think you know about me, but whatever it is, you're wrong. Now sit back and be quiet so I can think."

I did as Ethel asked, mainly because, for possibly the first time in my life, I was speechless. I thought about Zak and couldn't quite control the tear that slid down my cheek. He was going to be devastated. I hoped he would be able to get over my death and move on with his life. And Charlie . . . Charlie wouldn't understand why I never returned for him. I hated to think of him sitting by the door, waiting for his best friend, who would never come back to him. And how in the heck were Levi and Ellie going to be able to manage their lives without my constant interference?

There was no way around it. I had to get out of there before we got to wherever it was we were going.

I noticed the lake to the left. I remembered passing close to it as we made our way from the airport to the tavern on that first night in Alaska. Were we headed for the airport? If we were I only had a minute or two to make my move. Ethel had set the gun down after the car had taken off. She was looking at her phone and not paying a whole lot of attention to me. I looked out the window at the passing scenery and the frigid lake. I knew what I needed to do. I wasn't thrilled about the idea, but it was my only chance. I noticed the bridge ahead and knew the time to act was now. As the car slowed to make its way across the narrow, icy surface, I opened the door and jumped out. I heard Ethel scream at the driver to stop as I rolled across the snow and dropped off the bridge into the icy water.

When I say icy I mean mind-numbingly freezing. I knew I only had seconds before Ethel showed up with her gun, so I used my legs to kick off and swam as deeply and quickly as I could manage. Luckily, I had been swimming in a lake fed by snowmelt my entire life. However, even with my experience I had less than a couple of minutes to find a place where there was enough cover to pull my way out of the water. My plan at that point hadn't evolved beyond freezing to death in the dense forest as opposed to freezing to death in the frigid lake. I really had no idea how I was going to get out of this alive, but I thought I'd get out of the lake and figure out the rest once I was safely on land.

I heard several shots splash into the water, and Ethel and her driver speaking to each other for a moment before they got back into the car and drove away. They probably assumed—quite correctly, I feared—that I would never survive my icy plunge.

Somehow I made my way out of the water and back to the road. It was a clear day, but the temperature still hovered just below freezing. I pulled my cell phone out of my pocket, which, thankfully, I'd encased in one of those waterproof cases. I asked Siri to call Zak. He didn't pick up. I didn't have the phone number of the inn or anyone else local, so I left a message and began to walk back toward the inn.

I knew that unless someone came along to pick me up I'd never make it. If I had been thinking clearly I would have called someone from home and had them call the inn on my behalf, but my mind was growing fuzzy and my body was becoming numb. I was on the verge of giving up and lying down on the soft blanket of snow when I heard what sounded an awful lot like dogs barking.

"Zak," I screamed with all my might.

I stopped to listen. At first I heard nothing, but then I saw the beautiful sight of Zak and Marty and two teams of dogs coming toward me.

"Oh my God, Zoe, what happened?" Zak dropped to his knees and hugged me to his body.

"Can't talk," I shivered.

Zak wrapped his heavy coat around me as Marty called Mary and instructed her to bring the truck.

"We need to get her warmed up," I heard Zak say from a distance.

"Put her in the sled and pile the dogs around her," Marty instructed. "Their body warmth should help quite a lot. Once Mary gets here we'll get her back to the inn and into a tub. I'm calling Jordan right now."

"Will she be okay?" Zak asked.

"Yeah, she'll be fine once we get her warmed up, but it's gonna be a bitch as she thaws out."

I'd like to go on record as saying that the feeling of millions of little needles being jabbed into every inch of your skin as the numbness fades and the feeling in your body starts to return isn't one I'd like to repeat. Ever.

"Am I going to live?" I asked Jordan, who had been waiting at the inn for me when I arrived.

"You are. Actually, once you warm up you'll be fine. I'll check you over for tissue damage, but I don't expect to find any."

"I appreciate your coming."

"It's what I do." Jordan smiled.

After what seemed like an eternity of agony, the needles stopped. I was transferred from the bathtub to the bed Zak and I shared at the inn. My little heat-sharing dog curled up next to me, looking more worried than I'd seen him for quite some time.

"Is it okay if I attend the party tonight?" I asked Jordan.

"I don't see why not, as long as you're feeling up to it. I'd ditch the dress and shoes and wear something warmer, though."

I looked across the room to where Jordan stood looking at my oh-so-sexy and expensive outfit, which was laid out across a chair. Suddenly, changing into a strapless dress and high heels didn't hold any appeal at all. Maybe I'd take a page from Orson's playbook and wear my flannel jammies to the party.

"Orson is here," Jordan said, as if she'd read my mind. "He'd like to speak to you if you're up to it."

"Give me a minute to put on every piece of clothing I own and I'll be down."

"Okay. I'll see you tonight." Jordan turned to leave. "Oh, and Zoe: good reflexes in a tough situation. If you ever want to leave Ashton Falls I can pretty much guarantee you a spot on the team."

"Thanks." I grinned. "That means a lot."

Chapter 14

Neverland was packed. It seemed everyone in town was out to ring in the new year at the only place in town that was actually having a party. The music was provided by a local band that was better than you'd expect, and Serge had outdone himself with a display of finger foods that looked almost too good to eat.

"Serge really knows how to put out a spread," Zak commented as he picked up a crab-stuffed pastry. Zak had been glued to my side ever since my very unfortunate abduction.

"The food really is exceptional. I wonder if he'd be willing to share some of his recipes. There are several items that would be perfect for the appetizer menu at Ellie's Beach Hut."

"I guess it couldn't hurt to ask him. Do you need anything?" Zak asked.

"Maybe something to drink."

"Okay. Wait here and I'll be right back."

I looked around the room after Zak walked away. Harmony had done a nice job with the decorations, adding silver and light blue to the Christmas décor that was still in place. The room was warm and cozy with accents of the year gone by mixed with new additions that spoke of rebirth and hope. I waved to Jordan, who waved back and started across the room toward me.

"How are you feeling?" Jordan had on a beautiful gold dress that made me sorry I'd decided on warm slacks, a long sleeved blouse, and sturdy boots.

"Much better, thanks to you."

"I didn't really do anything; you just needed to warm up."

"Be that as it may, I was very glad to have you there."

Jordan shrugged. "I do what I can, but at times it's difficult without a real hospital."

"Is the lack of such a facility due to a lack of funding?" I asked.

"In a nutshell. Medical equipment is expensive, and if we opened a hospital we'd need staff around the clock, which would be an additional expense. Moosehead is lucky enough to have a few very generous patrons like Harley Medford who have volunteered to provide part of the resources we need to get started if we can put a steady revenue source in place to cover ongoing expenses."

"Chloe mentioned that someone by the name of Harley was back in town. Didn't he donate the building for the animal shelter?"

"Yeah, that's the guy. He's over there, talking to Harmony."

I looked across the room to where Jordan was pointing. The guy was a babe. Were all the men in this town good-looking? Maybe it was the clean air and water.

"Harley and a few others are helping me come up with a plan that might earn us some private grant money, so maybe by the next time you come for a visit we'll have an upgraded facility. Of course, after your experience this afternoon, I'd imagine you won't be too anxious to come back any time soon."

"Actually, I'd like to come back in spite of my brush with death. Moosehead is a wonderful town filled with friendly, caring people."

"Mostly you're correct. Moosehead is filled with wonderful people. By the way, how did the interview with Orson go?"

"It went fine. I'm pretty sure he's completely over his head with this one, but now that Ethel is gone there isn't much he can do about bringing her to justice for Carter Christianson's murder. He's going to keep an eye on the inn to make certain she doesn't come back for her stuff, but I sort of doubt she will. I suggested that he contact the feds, given the fact that she was responsible for a highly respected reporter's death, and he said he planned to do so."

"Yeah, that's a good idea. I do find I'm interested in finding out who Ethel really is and what she was doing at the inn."

"Now that Zak has a photo of her without her old lady makeup, he's going to work on finding out who she is. He's pretty good at getting to the bottom of things like that. I'll let you know."

"Thanks." Jordan smiled. "I'd like that."

I spoke to Jordan for a few more minutes and then she moved on to say hi to her sister, who had shown up with her husband. If I remembered correctly, Jordan's sister had two or three young children. It had occurred to me on more than one occasion that being an only child, at least until Harper was born, meant that I would never have the opportunity to be an aunt. By the time Harper got around to getting married and having children, I'd be a very old aunt, but I supposed that was better than not being an aunt at all.

I was headed toward the bar to see what was keeping Zak when Harmony, dressed in a simple wool skirt and knee-high boots, intercepted me.

"I checked on the animals a little while ago," she informed me. "Charlie is having a great time playing with Sitka."

I hadn't planned to bring Charlie to the party because I knew the tavern would be loud and crowded, but he'd sensed there was something amiss, so I hated to leave him alone in our room. Luckily, Harmony had offered a perfect compromise when she suggested that I leave him in her upstairs apartment with Sitka and Whiskey, which would allow me to check on him whenever I felt the need.

"Thanks. I appreciate your suggesting that I bring him over. I hated to leave him alone in the inn after what happened today."

"It's no problem; he's always welcome. I passed Zak on my way over to you. It looks like he's having an intense conversation with Jake."

"Zak wants to find out who Ethel really is. He's determined to bring her to justice for what she almost did to me. Personally, I just want to move on from the whole thing."

"I guess I don't blame you. It has to have been a traumatic experience. I can't even imagine having a gun pointed at me."

"It's not fun, but it wasn't the first time."

Harmony frowned. "What do you mean, it wasn't the first time?"

"Let's just say this wasn't the first time my tendency to snoop has ended up getting me almost dead. I'm getting better at escaping, though. I guess practice really does make perfect."

Harmony laughed. "I hope you're kidding. There's so much about you I really don't know. We should go to lunch and just chat. How long will you be in Moosehead?"

"Actually, we're going home tomorrow. I'd love to stay longer, but Ashton Falls has its own unsolved murder that needs solving."

Harmony chuckled. "Maybe you need to take a sabbatical from sleuthing."

"You know, I think you might be right about that."

Chapter 15

New Year's Day

I yawned as I looked at the bedside clock. It was three a.m. We'd only been back from the party for a couple of hours. Zak was sitting at the desk doing something on his computer.

"Can't sleep?" I asked as I leaned up onto one elbow.

"Sorry. I didn't mean to wake you. And you're right; I can't sleep. I keep thinking about Ethel, or whatever her real name is, and the fact that she almost killed you. She's a dangerous woman who needs to be caught."

I sat up in the bed. Charlie adjusted his position and then went back to sleep. The poor little guy was exhausted after his long night of playing with Sitka.

"I don't disagree that the woman needs to be found, but I don't see what we can do in the middle of the night. Come back to bed."

"Actually, I was about to when I stumbled across something," Zak said. "I'm just not sure exactly what it means."

I got up, pulled on my robe and slippers, and walked over to the desk where Zak sat. "What'd you find?" I asked as I leaned an arm on his shoulder.

"I tied into my desktop at home and ran the photo of the younger Ethel through the facial recognition software I have. I haven't come up with a name yet, but I have come up with some additional photos. In each of these photos the woman is standing on a street corner as if waiting to cross. The photos were taken with a zoom lens from quite a distance, so I'm pretty sure Carter Christianson didn't want Ethel to know he was watching her. This is one of the photos that wasn't in Carter's case."

Zak pulled up a photo of a very exclusive and fancy party. "See her there in the background?" Zak pointed at a face among the crowd.

"Oh, yeah; that's her. So what is she doing there?"

"The party was a reception held at an art gallery in Moscow. The thing I find the most interesting is that the man Ethel is talking to works for Homeland Security."

I frowned. "So she's a spy?"

"If I had to guess I'd say she's some sort of an informant. The fact that she was going to kill you tells me that she isn't entirely on the up and up. I found another photo of the woman in the crowd after a bombing. She's simply standing in the background watching, and she really doesn't stand out as suspicious. In fact, if I'd been looking at the photo in an attempt to pick out the person responsible, I'm pretty sure I wouldn't even have noticed her."

"So she's a terrorist?" I asked.

"Maybe. I don't know yet. There seem to be a lot of things that don't add up at this point. I really need to get into Carter's computer to see if he had some notes on the woman. He must have had a reason for following her."

I leaned against Zak's chair. "So what *are* we going to do about the photos and computer?" I asked. "Should we turn them over to Orson?"

"I've scanned the photos so I have copies, so turning the originals over to Orson is fine. I have a feeling he'll be getting help from the higher-ups once the holiday is over, now that Ethel has been exposed as Carter's killer. But I'd hate to hand over the laptop unless I can get in and copy the hard drive."

"Okay, so we need to come up with the password. What do we know about him? Was he married? Did he have pets or kids?"

Zak typed in some commands. "No on all accounts."

"I suppose you tried one, two, three, four and a, b, c, d?"

Zak just rolled his eyes.

"My password on my bank account is 'incorrect password.'"

Zak looked at me with raised eyebrows. "Your password is 'incorrect password'?"

"Yeah. I kept forgetting it, and every time I'd get the message that I had an incorrect password I'd be prompted to change my password, and then I'd forget that one as well. Finally, I decided that if I made my password 'incorrect password' I'd always have a clue."

"Your logic is infallible, but that's a terrible password. You really should change it."

"To what?"

"I don't know; we'll figure one out later."

Zak began typing again. His search pulled up a lot of stuff, including information on the places Carter'd worked and articles he'd written. There were tons of photos of him in locations all over the world. The man certainly had lived an interesting life. Zak quickly scanned through the photos, but none really stood out.

"Wait," I said. "Go back."

Zak went back two photos to the image I'd indicated, of a much younger Carter standing next to a German shepherd who had just competed in some sort of agility trial. "Can you find out who the dog is?"

Zak typed in some commands. "His name is—or I guess I should say was, since the photo is twenty years old—Tuckerman."

"Try Tuckerman as the password," I suggested.

"I doubt a man of Carter's experience would use his dog's name as a password."

"Just try it," I insisted.

Zak turned to the computer I'd found in Carter's room. He logged on and tried Tuckerman as the password. "Doesn't work," he informed me.

"Try Tuck or Tucker."

"Too short. It needs to be at least eight digits."

"Okay, try Tuckerdog."

Zak tried it. "Still no good."

"How about Tuckster?"

Zak just looked at me. "I doubt he called his dog Tuckster."

"Just try it."

Zak did, but it was still no go.

I looked at the photo again. The man and dog looked like they were competing in the event as some sort of dog/handler team. I could tell the pair were deeply bonded. I looked for a name on his tag or some other indication of what he might have called the dog outside of competition.

"Try Tuckerbuddy."

Zak frowned but did as I suggested. "Well, what do you know? Tuckerbuddy it is. How did you know?"

I smiled. "I knew the moment I saw Carter with the dog that they had a special bond. I just had to figure out his nickname for his best friend."

Zak whistled when the desktop appeared. "There are a lot of files here. It's going to take a long time to go through all of them."

"So what are we going to do?" I asked.

"I'm going to download the files. There's no way we'll have time to go through them all tonight, and Coop is coming for us in just over three hours," Zak said with a glance at the clock. "We should get packed up so we're ready. We can sleep on the plane if we need to."

The flight back to Ashton Falls was uneventful and, thankfully, the landing was smooth and steady. We'd left Zak's truck at the airport, so after we transferred Charlie and our luggage from the jet to the truck we headed back up the mountain. I would miss Harmony and the others, but I was glad to be home.

"So what did you find out while I was sleeping?" I asked Zak as we wound our way up the mountain. I knew he'd been digging through the files he'd downloaded during the long flight home.

"Carter had reason to believe that Ethel—whose name is really Claudia Lotherman, by the way—was some sort of government informant. He managed to establish a relationship with a woman who used to be Claudia's roommate. Claudia and this former roommate, who he never identified by name, maintained a close friendship, so more often than not she knew where Claudia was off to. Carter began following Claudia when she ventured overseas in order to get proof that she was meeting with people who would be considered enemies of the US. He realized that she had developed an extensive network of relationships that tended to get her invitations to upscale parties all over the world. Again, initially, he saw this as a means of gaining access to parties where there would be high-level officials."

"Like the one she attended at the embassy."

"Exactly." Zak slowed as we reached the summit and began working our way toward the lake and Ashton Falls. I could tell it had snowed quite a bit while we'd been gone. I couldn't wait to get up on the mountain to try out my new snowboard.

"So how did she get all of these men to escort her to these functions in the first place?" I asked.

"Claudia is a master of disguise. She was able to transform herself into whatever type of woman her research told her would appeal to the man she had targeted."

"Wow; that seems so unreal. You'd think a person's true age would come through."

"She had us convinced she was an eighty-year-old woman," Zak pointed out. "After reading Carter's notes, I went back and looked through the photos and realized she wasn't only the fifty-year-old brunette we picked out in several of the photos but also the twenty-five-year-old blonde and the forty-year-old Asian woman who were present in other photos as well."

"Fascinating."

"It really is," Zak agreed.

"So was there anything in Carter's files that would have linked Claudia and Gary?" I asked. "I know he died of natural causes, but the fact that he was in Moosehead snooping around at the same time that both Carter and Claudia were in town can't be a coincidence."

"It turns out it wasn't. Once I started to put things together I called a guy I know who works for the CIA."

"You know someone who works for the CIA?"

"I worked on a software issue with him a few years back. Anyway, while you were snoring away I forwarded him a photo of Gary. It turns out he was one of their operatives who was in Moosehead to track down Claudia, who was stealing government secrets and selling them to the highest bidder."

"So where does Devon fit into all of this?" I figured there had to be a connection. It would be too strange if there wasn't. The odds of Gary just happening to have a photo of Devon taken two weeks before he died and there not being a connection seemed astronomical.

"According to my source, Devon, whose real name is Trenton Goldman, was initially involved in military intelligence. It seems he has an IQ that's off the charts. The military tricked him into building a software program he believed would be used for humanitarian purposes but ended up being a weapon. Trenton became so disenchanted that he went AWOL."

"I'm guessing that's when he changed his name to Devon and moved to Moosehead."

"Exactly. What better place to hide out? The thing was that Gary tracked him down but initially couldn't prove Trenton and Devon were the same person, so he established a friendship with the man in order to get his proof. When Devon found out what was going on he decided to disappear."

"But he must have reestablished a relationship with Gary at some point if Gary had a photo of him."

"It appears so. My hunch is that Gary and Devon came to some sort of an agreement between themselves. I'm going to go out on a limb and state that the agreement they worked out concerning Devon's status as AWOL doesn't extend to the military as a whole, which would explain why Devon never reappeared. I'm sure he has a new alias and a new life now."

"So what now?"

"First I'm going to forward everything I have to my CIA contact so he can track down Claudia and put her behind bars, where she deserves to be, and then I'm going to take you home and we're going to open a bottle of champagne, take a romantic hot tub, and break in the new year the way every newly engaged couple should."

"Levi and Elli are at the house," I reminded him.

"Oh, yeah. I forgot about that. I guess we can sneak the champagne up to our room, feign exhaustion so that we can turn in early, and then climb into our big Jacuzzi tub."

"Sounds good." I glanced at Charlie, who was asleep on the backseat next to Zak's computer.

"So exactly how long do you think Levi and Ellie will be staying with us?"

"Levi is probably fine to go home if he wants to, but there's no way Ellie will be able to stay in the boathouse until her cast comes off. She certainly won't be able to climb the stairs to the bedroom. I guess she'll have to stay with us for several weeks at least, unless she decides to go to Levi's. The thing is that Levi is going to be pretty busy with his new assignment at the high school, so he won't be home to help her out."

"I didn't want to bring this up just yet," Zak began, "but I have to go out of town for a couple of weeks. The guy I was working with while we were in Alaska is having some issues I can't deal with long distance. Considering I'll be gone, maybe it would be best if Ellie just stayed on at the house. She can keep you company."

I have to admit I wasn't thrilled Zak was going to be away, but he'd somehow managed to stay home for the past couple of months, so I knew I really shouldn't complain.

"Okay, I'll suggest it to her." I tried for my best supportive fiancée smile.

"I've been thinking about the future," Zak said as we made our way through town. "I feel like I should try to work out a way to stay closer to home now that we're getting married. Traveling used to be fine, but now I find it tedious. I'm actually thinking about taking on a partner I can train to handle most of the legwork. I'd really like to be able to take the entire summer off."

"A partner?" I asked. I couldn't help but remember Zak's former partner, who looked like a supermodel.

"There's a guy who works for one of the big software firms I've dealt with a few times. He's smart and ambitious and I think we'd get along okay. If you don't have a problem with it, I think I might call him to see if he's at all open to the idea."

I turned to stare at Zak. "You're asking me if I have a problem with you taking on a partner?"

"Of course. You're going to be my wife. The decisions I make effect both of us."

"But it's *your* business," I pointed out.

"Only for a few more months, and then it'll be *our* business. So what do you say? Do you want to take on a partner? If after our phone conversation the guy is interested, I thought we could fly him out to talk to him."

"If it helps to keep you closer to home I'm all for it."

I thought about what Zak had said about his business being our business and his house being our house. Suddenly I wondered what I brought to the table.

"Zak?"

"Yeah?"

"Do you think we should get a prenup? I mean, you do have a *lot* of money."

Zak looked at me. "Are you planning to leave me and take everything I have?"

"Of course not."

"Then I don't think a prenup is necessary. Besides, everything I've earned I've earned for us."

"For us? But you made your money long before we started dating."

Zak pulled into our driveway and stopped the truck. He turned to face me. "When I met you in the seventh grade and you got so adorably outraged when I beat you in that mathathon, I decided Zoe Donovan was the girl I was going to marry. I've never lost sight of that. I knew I just needed to give you time to warm up to the idea, so I gave you some space. But I want you to know that every decision I've ever made I made for us and the future I was determined to someday have."

I wanted to say something, but I found myself completely speechless.

"So about that champagne . . ." Zak smiled.

Have I mentioned that I love this man?

Recipes

It's football playoffs at our house as I'm gathering recipes, so I decided to use game-day treats as my theme this month. I hope you enjoy them as much as the men in my house do.

Herb and Bacon Cheese Ball

Apricot Cheese Ball (contributed by Michele Gray)

Chicken Artichoke Dip

Chipped Beef Dip

Buffalo Chicken Quesadillas (contributed by Amy Brantley)

Beefy Nachos

Pumpkin Spice Pull-Apart Bread (contributed by Jade Knueppel)

Wyoming Buffalo Chips (contributed by Janel Flynn)

And for the doggie in your life: Nothing Better than Sweet Potato and Peanut Butter Treats (contributed by Joanne Kocourek)

Herb and Bacon Cheese Ball

12 oz. cream cheese, softened
6 pieces bacon, cooked crisp and crumbled
1 can (4 oz.) diced green chilies
1 tbs. chopped garlic
1 tbs. chopped fresh basil
1 tbs. chopped chives
1 cup grated Parmesan cheese
1 cup grated Jack cheese
1 cup grated cheddar cheese
2 tsp. horseradish
⅔ cup chopped almonds

Mix all ingredients except almonds in a bowl. I just use my hands to mix everything together. Form a ball. Lay almonds on a breadboard. Roll cheese ball in almonds until coated.

Wrap in plastic wrap and chill overnight. Serve with crackers.

Apricot Cheese Ball
Contributed by Michele Gray

1 (8 oz.) cream cheese, softened
20 dried apricots
2 heaping tbs. apricot preserves
1 tsp. vanilla
1 tsp. sugar
Chopped walnuts

Chop apricots. In a mixing bowl, add all ingredients and mix well. Roll into a ball. Then roll in chopped walnuts or pecans. Wrap in plastic wrap and refrigerate overnight.

I make this at my Christmas parties and it's always a hit. I actually double the recipe so I get two cheese balls. ENJOY!

Chicken Artichoke Dip

Combine in large bowl:
2 large chicken breasts, cooked and cubed
2 cups artichoke hearts, chopped
8 oz. cream cheese, softened
I cup grated Parmesan cheese
1 cup Pepper Jack cheese, grated
1 cup cheddar cheese, grated
14 oz. diced green chiles (Ortega)
1 cup mayonnaise
Salt and pepper to taste

Pour into 9 x 13 pan. Top with additional grated cheese (as much as you want).

Bake at 350 degrees until bubbly (about 45 minutes).

Serve with chips, crackers, French bread slices, or tortillas.

Chipped Beef Dip

16 oz. sour cream
8 oz. cream cheese, softened
1 can jalapeños (or more, if you like it really hot)
1 large jar dried beef, rinsed and chopped

Mix ingredients above. Bake at 350 degrees for 1 hour.

Serve with French bread squares or tortilla chips.

Buffalo Cheese Quesadillas

Contributed by Amy Brantley

1 lb. cooked boneless chicken breasts or chicken
tenderloins, shredded
Frank's Buffalo Sauce
4 large flour tortillas
8 oz. Colby-Jack cheese, sliced
8 oz. Pepper Jack cheese, sliced
4–8 oz. blue cheese to taste

Mix shredded chicken with hot sauce to taste.

Cover half a tortilla with a quarter of all the cheeses
and a quarter of the chicken. Fold and place on a large
nonstick cookie sheet.

Repeat the process with the remaining ingredients.

Bake at 350 degrees for 15 to 20 minutes, or until the
cheese is completely melted.

Allow to cool for 2 to 3 minutes before cutting into
wedges.

Serve with ranch dressing for dipping.

Beefy Nachos

Make meat the day before your football gathering.

Trim all fat off boneless rib roast (size depends on amount of meat desired). Season with salt, pepper, and garlic powder. Place in slow cooker. Cover meat with store-bought salsa, either hot or mild, depending on preference.

Cook on high until meat begins to pull apart. Continue to shred meat as it cooks. When it's completely done (cooking time depends on amount of meat and heat of slow cooker, but about 8 hours), spoon meat from sauce with slotted spoon.

Refrigerate.

Next day:

Layer tortilla chips on cookie sheet. Cover with grated cheese; I use sharp cheddar and Jack, but you can use whatever.

Place cookie sheet under broiler with heat set on low.

Reheat the meat on stove or in microwave. When cheese is melted on tortilla chips cover with meat—be sure it's drained of excess fluid—and serve with sour cream, guacamole, diced tomatoes, or whatever you'd like to add.

Pumpkin Spice
Pull-Apart Bread

Contributed by Jade Knueppel

2 (16.3 oz.) cans buttermilk biscuits

Sugar/Spice mix:
½ cup sugar
1 tsp. pumpkin pie spice
¼ tsp. cinnamon

Filling:
8 oz. cream cheese
2 tsp. vanilla
¼ cup sugar

Glaze:
½ cup melted butter
½ cup packed brown sugar

Preheat oven to 350 degrees. Spray bundt pan. Combine pumpkin spice, sugar, and cinnamon.

Open biscuit cans and cut each biscuit in half; you will have 32 pieces.

In small bowl mix cream cheese, vanilla, and ½ cup sugar.

Press each biscuit half into a disc and put some filling in the middle (about a tsp. and a half) and seal into a ball. Then coat in sugar/spice mix. Layer biscuit balls in bundt pan.

Mix melted butter and brown sugar, then pour over biscuits and bake 40 minutes or until dough is cooked through.

Wyoming Buffalo Chips

Contributed by Janel Flynn

This recipe was one I used to make with my mother growing up. Not to mention my brother and I got into food fights with it. Better than the average "monster" cookie.

1 cup margarine
1 cup Crisco
2 cups sugar
2 cups brown sugar
4 eggs
2 tbs. vanilla
4 cups flour
2 tsp. baking soda
2 tsp. baking powder
2 cups oatmeal
2 cups corn flakes
1 cup coconut
1 cup nuts
6 oz. chocolate chips
6 oz. butterscotch chips
6 oz. peanut butter chips

We added raisins and mint chocolate chips also.

CREAM MARGARINE, CRISCO, AND ADD SUGARS AND CREAM THEM TOGETHER. ADD EGGS AND VANILLA; MIX VERY WELL.

SIFT FLOUR, SODA, AND POWDER AND ADD TO MIXTURE.

ADD REMAINING INGREDIENTS. DROP ON COOKIE SHEET WITH AN ICE CREAM SCOOP.

BAKE 15-17 MINUTES AT 350 DEGREES. IF YOU MAKE THE COOKIES SMALLER, DO NOT BAKE AS LONG.

Nothing Better than Sweet Potatoes and Peanut Butter Treats for Dogs

Submitted by Joanne Kocourek

1½ tbs. flax (plus 2 tbs. water)
1 sweet potato
1 egg
¼ cup coconut milk
½ cup peanut butter
½ cup coconut flour (you can try increasing the amount to make the batter thicker)

Preheat oven to 350 degrees.

Combine the flax and water in a bowl and let it sit so that the flax makes a paste.

Cut up the sweet potato and boil until soft. Let cool, remove skins, and mash.

Combine all ingredients in a mixer and mix well.

Line a cooking sheet with parchment paper. Drop batter onto paper in the size you prefer.

Bake for 15 minutes, then take a wooden spoon and lightly press down on each cookie to flatten out any sharp areas. (If the cookies have sharp areas, they could scrape the top of your doggie's mouth.)

Bake another 20–25 minutes. Pull out and let cool.

Store chilled in the fridge. I'm sure they would last a couple of days on the counter, but they will last a lot longer inside the fridge.

Our dogs LOVE these treats. Of course, we have four nonfood discriminating dogs! Our granddaughter thought these were cookies and loved them. They are safe for young humans as well.

Books by Kathi Daley

Come for the murder, stay for the romance.

Buy them on Amazon today.

Zoe Donovan Cozy Mystery:

Halloween Hijinks
The Trouble With Turkeys
Christmas Crazy
Cupid's Curse
Big Bunny Bump-off
Beach Blanket Barbie
Maui Madness
Derby Divas
Haunted Hamlet
Turkeys, Tuxes, and Tabbies
Christmas Cozy
Alaskan Alliance
Matrimony Meltdown – April 2015
Soul Surrender – May 2015
Heavenly Honeymoon – June 2015

Zoe Donovan Cookbook

Ashton Falls Cozy Cookbook

Paradise Lake Cozy Mystery:

Pumpkins in Paradise
Snowmen in Paradise
Bikinis in Paradise
Christmas in Paradise
Puppies in Paradise – February 2015

Whales and Tails Cozy Mystery:

Romeow and Juliet – January 2015
The Mad Catter – Febraury 2015
Grims Furry Tail – March 2015

Road to Christmas Romance:

Road to Christmas Past

Kathi Daley lives with her husband, kids, grandkids, and Bernese mountain dogs in beautiful Lake Tahoe. When she isn't writing, she likes to read (preferably at the beach or by the fire), cook (preferably something with chocolate or cheese), and garden (planting and planning, not weeding). She also enjoys spending time on the water when she's not hiking, biking, or snowshoeing the miles of desolate trails surrounding her home.

Kathi uses the mountain setting in which she lives, along with the animals (wild and domestic) that share her home, as inspiration for her cozy mysteries.

Stay up to date with her newsletter, *The Daley Weekly*. There's a link to sign up on both her Facebook page and her website, or you can access the sign-in sheet at: http://eepurl.com/NRPDf

Visit Kathi:
Facebook at Kathi Daley Books,
www.facebook.com/kathidaleybooks

Kathi Daley Books Group Page –
https://www.facebook.com/groups/569578823146850/

Kathi Daley Recipe Exchange -
https://www.facebook.com/groups/752806778126428/

Webpage - www.kathidaley.com

E-mail - kathidaley@kathidaley.com

Recipe Submission E-mail –
kathidaleyrecipes@kathidaley.com

Goodreads:
https://www.goodreads.com/author/show/7278377.
Kathi_Daley

Twitter at Kathi Daley@kathidaley -
https://twitter.com/kathidaley

Tumblr - http://kathidaleybooks.tumblr.com/

Amazon Author Page -
http://www.amazon.com/Kathi-
Daley/e/B00F3BOX4K/ref=sr_tc_2_0?qid=141823
7358&sr=8-2-ent

Pinterest - http://www.pinterest.com/kathidaley/

39118443R00113

Made in the USA
Lexington, KY
07 February 2015